"Let me take you home."

Micah Steele's voice was so soft Delphi jerked her head up in surprise. Her mouth opened to utter the words "get lost" but they never emerged.

"You're staring at me, Mr. Steele," Delphi responded tartly, her eyes turning away from his fixed gaze.

"I just want to take you home. I've wanted to meet you for a long time, Delphi . . . and stop calling me Mr. Steele. Micah is the name," he said firmly, his face coming down to hers, his black panther eyes, flecked with brown and gold, seeming to pin her to his side like a butterfly to a board. His lips just teased hers, but he could feel his heart jump when they touched. It had been so long since a woman had reached him like this one had. The kiss deepened, and when he felt her stiffen as if to draw back, he pulled her hard against him, the velvet texture of her mouth making his pulse race . . .

WHAT ARE *LOVESWEPT* ROMANCES?

They are stories of true romance and touching emotion. We believe those two very important ingredients are constants in our highly sensual and very believable stories in the *LOVESWEPT* line. Our goal is to give you, the reader, stories of consistently high quality that may sometimes make you laugh, sometimes make you cry, but are always fresh and creative and contain many delightful surprises within their pages.

Most romance fans read an enormous number of books. Those they truly love, they keep. Others may be traded with friends and soon forgotten. We hope that each *LOVESWEPT* romance will be a treasure—a "keeper." We will always try to publish

*LOVE STORIES YOU'LL NEVER FORGET
BY AUTHORS YOU'LL ALWAYS REMEMBER*

The Editors

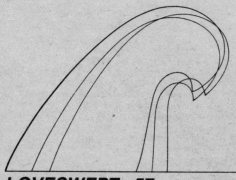

LOVESWEPT • 57

Helen Mittermeyer
Unexpected Sunrise

 BANTAM BOOKS
TORONTO • NEW YORK • LONDON • SYDNEY • AUCKLAND

UNEXPECTED SUNRISE

A Bantam Book / August 1984

The poem Colours by Yevgeny Yevtushenko from Yevtushenko:
SELECTED POEMS, trans. Robin Milner-Gulland and Peter
Levi (Penguin Modern European Poets 1962) p. 77.
Copyright © 1962 by Robin Milner-Gulland and Peter Levi.

LOVESWEPT and the wave device are trademarks of
Bantam Books, Inc.

ISBN 0-553-21640-6

Published simultaneously in the United States and Canada

Bantam Books are published by Bantam Books, Inc. Its
trademark, consisting of the words "Bantam Books" and the
portrayal of a rooster, is Registered in U.S. Patent and Trademark Office and in other countries. Marca Registrada. Bantam
Books, Inc., 666 Fifth Avenue, New York, New York 10103.

PRINTED IN THE UNITED STATES OF AMERICA

O   0 9 8 7 6 5 4 3 2 1

One

Delphi Reed didn't want to go back to the Battersons' office for the kickoff party for the Sunlight Cosmetics campaign. She'd put in a long day at Wolf's studio and would have preferred to go straight home, but Selma and George Batterson had pleaded and cajoled until she agreed to stop by for one drink.

The Battersons were good friends as well as the owners of the modeling agency where Delphi, born Delphinium Reed of Seneca County in midstate New York, got most of her well-paying assignments. Modeling on a free-lance basis wasn't the safest way to handle the business, but it satisfied Delphi's sense of independence.

Selma's outer office was crowded with laughing people. It seemed as though everyone in midtown Manhattan was there. It was still just two days into December and there had been no snow, but there was a holiday feeling in the air.

Delphi saw Micah Aristotle Steele the moment she pressed into the throng. And she almost turned and left. Not that she really knew him, or even had been introduced to him, but she appeared in many commercials for his companies and had heard a great deal about him. In fact, gossip surrounded the man like a cape and, fact or fiction, the talk about Steele consistently delineated the type of man Delphi didn't happen to like. She avoided gatherings that included people of his ilk.

"Delphi, love, how wonderful . . ." Edgar Batterson, blinking myopically through heavy horn-rimmed lenses, grabbed her hand. Edgar was Selma's brother-in-law and was alleged to play a minor role in the agency. Privately, Delphi felt it was Edgar's business acumen that kept Batterson's near the top in the highly competitive world of the modeling agencies. "Sorry, Delphi." Edgar nodded his head toward Steele, who was still surrounded by a number of people. "We didn't know he was coming."

Delphi shrugged and smiled at the small-statured man, allowing him to lead her along the edge of the room. It was not Edgar's style to plow through the middle, but rather to do a perimeter approach to his objective. She took the drink offered by a waiter and studied the room through barely raised lashes. "Quite a crowd, even for Selma and George."

"Yes. The usual host of crocodiles hoping to feed on one another," Edgar said in a low voice, his eyes glinting with delight when laughter spilled from her lips. "You do have the most marvelous laugh, Del. It is your special charm, I think."

"What a flatterer you are." Delphi grinned at him. Edgar might be shy, but he was also a very straightforward individual and would not say anything he didn't mean.

She sipped at her champagne and wrinkled her nose.

When the hand reached out and took the glass from her, she followed the motion of the long, spatulate fingers that should have belonged to a pianist.

"You don't seem to like champagne. Let me get you something else." Micah Steele's voice cut between Edgar and Delphi like a velvet-encased machete. He turned to look at the smaller man. "Maybe you could get something that you know Miss Reed likes."

As Edgar turned away, Delphi took his arm. "I'll go with you, Edgar. Excuse us." She moved as fast as possible through the crowd, pushing Edgar in front of her, not stopping until they had made almost a complete turn around the room.

"Del, must you commit hara-kiri socially and right before my eyes?" Edgar panted as he wheeled to face her in front of a sideboard laden with canapés. "You *know* that was Steele. I pointed him out and apologized that he was here."

"Yes, I know . . . and I don't really give a damn."

"Foolish of you," Micah Steele drawled into her ear, making her jump. "You do work for me as Cassie the Computer Girl on television, as the lady lumberjack in the Acme Paper magazine ads, as the Gold Velvet Girl on the auto commercials—"

"I didn't know you had a piece of Stahl Auto Industries too," Delphi stated, her angry feelings put aside for a moment.

"Stahl Electronics Industries, Ltd., is the parent company for Steele Associates." Micah Steele said the words with a hard twist to his mouth, his black eyes narrowed on her. "My grandfather changed Stahl to Steele to Americanize his German name," he explained in frigid tones. "Here, I brought you a Chablis. Perhaps you would prefer it."

"I would prefer the seltzer water my friend Edgar is getting for me." Delphi let her eyes slide toward Edgar, who nodded and signaled to a white and black garbed waiter, mouthing Delphi's order to him. The man nodded and scurried away.

"I see." Steele set down the glass of wine on a nearby table, not even bothering to steady it when it wobbled on the corner of the wooden top.

"Lord, be careful, can't you. . . ." Delphi's hand shot out and clutched at the glass, some of the liquid spilling on the long sleeve of her apple-green dress, which was one shade lighter than her silvery green eyes.

"Leave the damn thing!" Micah growled, no longer bothering to hide his anger at Delphi. His hooded panther eyes, so black, rayed with brown and gold, sparkled with emotion.

"Easy for you to say since it isn't your table." She looked up at him, not hiding her anger either as she mopped at the sodden sleeve.

He was as angry as she, but now humor touched his mouth. "Your eyes are the color of maple leaves in the rain . . . sensational!" He looked down for a moment at her hand still mopping at the wet spot. "Forget that. I'll buy you a new dress tomorrow, tonight if you like. Come home with me. We'll get the dress—"

"I'll be right back, Mr. Steele. I must go to the powder room. Edgar, be a dear and show me where it is." Delphi stared hard at him when he opened his mouth, she was sure, to tell her that the powder room was still where it had always been.

"Uh, fine, come this way, Del. Excuse us, Micah."

"Of course," Steele responded, his manner urbane.

They walked down the hall leading from the office to the Battersons' apartment. At a bedroom door, Delphi whirled on Edgar. "Thanks. Tell Selma and George that I had a sudden headache or something. I have no intention of going back into that room with that . . . that shark."

Edgar followed her into the bedroom and closed the door and leaned against it. "You do have a tendency to attack Zeus, don't you, my dear?" Edgar shook his head, his smile stretching in admiration as he watched her in the mirror. "All that red hair twisted on top of your head doesn't hide that glorious color. Is that where your temper comes from? God, most women would give their eyeteeth if Micah Steele followed them around the room at a gathering. Generally speaking, it is the other way around: they follow him." Edgar watched her as she straightened, her eyes meeting his in the glass. "You look like a six-foot-tall Christmas angel in that green silk dress and you have great legs," Edgar mused dispassionately. "Of course that's one of the reasons you get those stocking commercials. Even at thirty years old, you still are some looker." Edgar assessed her. "You can go on working for another ten years at least."

"Or retire, thanks to you . . . and those investments you've made for me. Of course the royalties from the book you encouraged me to write on diet don't hurt the investment picture, either."

"Ah, yes, *The Model's Diet to Good Health*," Edgar said, obviously pleased. Delphi's book had been published the year before and was selling very well.

She looked at the door, then tilted her head at Edgar. "I think the coast must be clear. Micah Steele has a low threshold of interest when it comes to women. He has so many to choose from."

"Don't bait him, Del." Edgar shook his finger at her, even as he opened the door to the bedroom. "He's a very rough man to tangle with. Stronger people, more powerful people than you have tried and not succeeded."

Edgar walked her to the door and promised he would make her excuses to Selma and George.

Delphi pressed the elevator button.

"I've already summoned the lift," Micah Steele said behind her, his British accent stronger than when he'd spoken to her before.

Delphi didn't turn around, only inclined her head to indicate that she had heard him.

"I'm following you home . . . or driving you home. Which is it?" Micah stepped into the elevator and stood next to her. "Did you drive?"

Delphi fumed, her eyes riveted on the numbers on the control panel lighting in sequence as the elevator went down. "I am taking a taxi."

When they reached the ground floor, Micah took her hand, restraining her, and she wasn't able to pry herself free.

"Let me take you home." His voice was so soft she jerked up her head in surprise.

Her mouth opened to utter the words "Get lost," but they didn't emerge.

He watched her, seeing the negative lift to her chin. She was so very beautiful, but he was used to seeing gorgeous women with skin that was as translucent as a pearl freshly taken from its shell. He had seen luminescent green eyes before, perhaps not quite that same silvery green. Tall, sylph-like women were a common enough occurrence in his life. So were long slender legs, with slim feet and ankles. His other hand came out to clasp her left hand between both of his. What was it that made her so unique besides her barely tamped fire, her independence? Was it that fragile bone structure that looked as if it could be crushed like a matchstick, yet revealed enough strength to make the world back down and like it?

"You're staring!" Delphi inhaled sharply, her eyes slipping away from his fixed gaze.

"I just want to drive you home. Perhaps we could have dinner together."

"No . . . I have other plans." Delphi wasn't lying. She had told Sam and Nora Griggs that she would watch their son Billy while they went to the Mostly Mozart concert.

"I see." Micah helped her into the limousine that had pulled up to the curb the moment they stepped from the building. A blustery wind caromed off the cement-and-steel building to buffet them with cold before the chauffeur could close the car door.

Delphi glanced at the plush interior of the back of the limousine. "The last time I traveled in one of these was when I went to my graduation ball at college. The dates hired a limo for the evening. I think it might have been grander than this. It was fun." She did not look at the man next to her, feeling safer when she kept her eyes on the chauffeur's cap.

"I've wanted to meet you for a long time, but the Battersons have managed to put me off," Micah said.

"At my orders." Delphi swallowed hard and forced herself to look at him. "I date friends of my own choosing."

"Anyone special at the moment?" Steele's voice was like his name. He held a pencil-slim black cigar in his hand that he quickly lifted to his lips and lit with a heavy gold lighter.

"My private life is my own and I have no need to discuss it—"

"Good. There's no one special or you would say so," Micah mused, a little irritated by the feeling of relief that flooded him.

"Mr. Steele," Delphi said, "I don't date men like—"

"You don't even know me. Don't judge me out of some preconceived notions of what you think I must be." Micah settled back against the silver velour upholstery.

"Must you interrupt every time I speak?" Delphi snapped.

He swung round to look at her in the flashing kaleidoscope of light caused by the myriad lights along the street. She was absolutely lovely, he thought. Her nose was so straight, classic . . . what the hell was the matter with him? He crushed out the cigar. There was something about her though, something elusive . . .

"Thank you," Delphi murmured.

"For what?" Micah hitched his body around so that he was facing her profile.

"For not smoking. I detest it." Delphi sniffed the air, sure sulfur fumes joined the cigar smoke as the man next to her stiffened and sucked in an angry breath.

"Dictatorial, aren't you?"

Delphi tensed, hating the smothering feeling she always had in the presence of high-powered men. She tried to avoid Steele's type of man. Once burned, twice shy was not a cliché to her. John was a vivid reminder of the truth of that maxim.

"Where the hell are you now? Who are you thinking of?" Steele demanded.

Delphi turned her head to see that they were pulling up in front of her apartment. The chauffeur came around to open the door, but Micah didn't move.

"Get out of my way, Steele. And I mean permanently!" The words were out before she really formulated them. Then it was her turn to stop breathing as she saw the black menace in Micah's panther eyes. She could feel her skin shrivel as she tried to draw back from him in the confines of the car.

In one quick move, he was out, stepping back, leaving it to the chauffeur to take her elbow and help her from the car.

Without another word, Delphi strode across the walk and up the steps to her converted brownstone. She co-owned the building with the Griggses; she had the top two floors; they had the bottom two.

She never looked back even when she heard the powerful car roar away from the curb as though somehow the machine had taken on the fury of its owner.

She stepped into the small elevator that would take her to the third-floor apartment. It was only seven-fifteen, but she felt as though it were midnight . . . and as though she'd been on the rack for days! The phone was ringing as she entered and she hurried to answer it. "Yes. Oh, sure. That would be great. Can I help you and Sam bring the things up here? No. Okay. I'll see you in a few minutes."

Delphi scurried around the apartment, collecting delicate items and sharp objects and putting them away to make the apartment safe for—and from—the ebullient but mischievous eighteen-month-old boy who was soon to visit. He was as dear to her as if he were her own. And his father, Sam, and mother, Nora, were like brother and sister to her. Her own parents were dead and she had been an only child. As far as she knew her only relative was an uncle in the town of Seneca Falls in upstate New York. She hadn't seen him in several years and the exchange of Christmas cards was the only regular connection between them. She felt a familiar ache in her chest for just a moment. She would never have a family of her own. She had vowed to herself that she wouldn't have children, wouldn't marry after her experience with John—the man she thought she had loved, the man whose baby she had carried, the man whom she had found in bed with another woman when he thought she was visiting her family.

Delphi shook her head to clear her cobwebby thoughts and hurried to answer the knock on the door. She was eager to see little Billy, the perfect antidote to bitter memories.

"Darling!" She reached for the chubby little boy with the sandy hair and light brown eyes. He chortled and threw himself forward out of his mother's arms to get to his "Duhwy."

"Heavens, Del, he's in rare form tonight." His harassed mother watched him slip from Delphi's embrace, balance with effort, then toddle across the pegged oak floor. He staggered and fell easily into the middle of the Bokhara rug that was the focal piece for the conversation area of Delphi's living room. "I'll understand if you pitch him out the window." Nora Griggs rolled her eyes at her smiling friend.

Both women looked toward the open doorway when they heard the elevator doors open, then crash. Sam struggled to get the Port-a-Crib and other paraphernalia needed for Billy out of the elevator and into Delphi's foyer. They ran to the beleaguered father's rescue.

"Phew," Sam said. "This kid requires more equipment to travel than the President of the United States."

Delphi chuckled, feeling at peace in the company of these people who were like family to her.

Micah Steele stood at the windowed wall of his penthouse and looked out over Manhattan's night-bright skyline. There was a double Irish whiskey in his hand and a restlessness in his soul. "What makes her tick?" he asked in a whisper. The darkness of the room was eerily shadowed by the light above a painting by Picasso over the mantel. Micah had been standing in the same position for the last half-hour, moving once to freshen his drink, but then returning to the spot to stare pensively through the glass. The panorama of dark sky and city lights looked like a handful of multicolored jewels thrown onto a piece of black velvet.

"Damn her!" Micah spun away from the window, sloshing some of the drink on his hand. He slammed the glass down on a rosewood parquet table and went out of the room, down the darkened hall to his library, not flipping a switch once to light his way, his silk dress socks making no sound on the thickly carpeted floor.

He flicked on the desk lamp and thumbed through the private phone directory he had there. DELPHI REED. There it was. He had looked up her name and number the first time he had seen her as Cassie the Computer Girl in one of his commercials. Since then, more than five months ago, he had been trying to meet her while managing to rid himself permanently of his mistress. It was a surface irritation that Delphi Reed had never been around when he wanted to meet her; it had been more deeply galling when he realized that the Battersons were deliberately keeping him away from her.

He poked his finger at her name and address in the directory. "So . . . I had to tell the Battersons that I wasn't coming to their party, then show up, to ensure that I would get to meet the elusive Delphi . . . and what do I find? An aloof, rather cold lady . . ." He jabbed his finger at her name once more. "And I don't like it."

He whirled and strode from the room, not bothering to turn off the light. He ran up the short flight of stairs to his bedroom, whipped through the informal clothing on one wall of his walk-in closet. Yanking off the rack a pair of dress jeans in café-au-lait color, he snatched a silk shirt to match. He dressed quickly and put on beige leather Docksides that he used on his boat *The Medea*, shrugged on a champagne-colored suede vest and a jacket. He shoved his car keys into the pocket, then he glanced at his watch when he descended in his private elevator to the underground garage. Nine-thirty. Even the frosty Miss Reed must still be up at such an early hour.

Delphi heaved a sigh of relief when she looked in on Billy. He was sound asleep in his Port-a-Crib, facedown, rump in the air, his huggy blanket clutched close to his body. "You are dynamite, angel boy, pure dynamite," Delphi whispered.

She backed out of her bedroom, closing the door with great care, then walked down the circular stairway to the foyer that opened onto the living room. An upstairs balcony overlooked the living area as well and provided an openness that was both airy and attractive.

She went into the kitchen. A long marble-topped counter separated the living and dining area from the kitchen, and oak cabinetry in the kitchen plus the continuation of the wood floors gave a homey smartness to the whole. Delphi loved the openness of her apartment and blessed the day a friend had talked her into investing some of her money in real estate. She had met the Griggses when the couple had come to look at the shabby brownstone the same day she had. After several meetings with them, the three had decided to buy the building in partnership.

The water had almost boiled for her tea when the

doorbell rang. "Just a minute," Del called out in a loud whisper as she turned off the kettle and hurried to the door, hoping Billy wouldn't waken. She fully intended to tell Sam and Nora to leave Billy with her for the rest of the evening. She flung open the door. "I didn't expect you until later—" Her voice faltered as her eyes traveled up the long muscular body of Micah Steele, a lock of his anthracite-black hair falling forward on his forehead as he leaned one shoulder on the doorjamb. "What are you doing here?" she gulped, feeling both threatened and excited as he looked her up and down, from her bare feet all the way up the turquoise terry-cloth sweatpants and shirt that she often wore for lounging and which she had owned for years.

"I like your hair down like that." His voice was a coarse velvet as though the fine texture of it had been damaged by smoke. "I hadn't realized it was so long . . . nor that it was so curly. May I come in?" He moved past her into the foyer.

"No. I don't entertain this late in the evening." Delphi felt as though butterflies had just flitted over every square inch of her skin. The man was a threat. Her mind cast about for ways to get him to leave even as she watched him stroll into the living room and look around.

"This is attractive. Did you have it done by a decorator?" He pulled a gold case from an inner pocket in his vest, touched a snap to open it.

"Ahem . . ." Delphi pointed to a sign in scrollwork: *Please do not smoke.*

Micah frowned at the sign, then at her. "You must lose friends very easily."

"I find that if people assume they can poison the atmosphere, they should be straightened out." She lifted her chin, determined not to be intimidated by him. It irked her that she felt such a fluttery feeling inside when he looked at her. She could feel her muscles tightening as she drew herself up to her full five feet ten inches . . . in socks. This was her home. "You were not invited here, Mr. Steele; if you don't like the house rules, leave." She flung the door wider and gestured with her hand.

"I'm not leaving," he barked, startling her when he flung the unlit cigar across the room, his hands hanging loose at his sides as though he would prepare himself for battle. "We are going to have a talk."

Delphi didn't close the door but she walked away from it toward the cigar in the corner. She bent down to pick it up, but his hand was there first, taking the cheroot, crumbling it in his fist, and staring at her.

"There, the housekeeping is done. Now sit down. I mean, *please* sit down," he amended when she opened her mouth to speak. "I am not leaving this apartment until we talk."

"I have nothing to say to you," Delphi began.

"Sit down!" he roared.

"Don't yell at me!" she shouted back, feeling her hands ball into fists.

He threw the remains of the cigar into a small tray on the ceramic coffee table.

"Dammit," he bellowed.

"Duhwy . . . Duhwy . . ." Billy wailed.

"Now look what you've done," Delphi grated out. "You wakened him with your shouting."

"Who?" Micah asked, his eyes wide with surprise.

"Billy," Delphi replied, sailing across the living room to the circular stairway and racing up to the second floor. She could feel Steele's eyes on her as she hurried across the balcony toward her bedroom doorway. "Here's Duhwy, darling. Hush, now, love." She picked the sleepy bundle up into her arms and cradled him against her.

"Man." Billy pointed, blinking, at a point over her shoulder.

Delphi looked around to see Micah standing at the head of the staircase, staring. "Would you mind waiting downstairs? I want to try to put him back to sleep." Not hesitating for his reply, she carried the baby to the bathroom, where she coaxed him to go to the bathroom, then had to lure him away from the water in the sink when he wanted to play.

It surprised her that Micah was still in the bedroom when she returned. She frowned at him.

"Don't make a fuss, Delphi. I'm used to children. I have two of my own, a boy and a girl, both grown." He smiled at the baby and held out his arms.

When Billy readily went into Steele's arms and played with the collar of Micah's silk shirt, Delphi ground her teeth. She watched him hold the child close to him and smile. He did have a wonderful smile. No wonder women buckled before him. And that dimple at the corner of his mouth . . . He oozed charm and Delphi wished she could rid herself of a prickling sensation when Micah looked up and smiled at her.

"He's a handsome boy, but he doesn't look like you."

"Ah . . . he resembles his father quite a bit," Delphi fibbed by omission, knowing that Micah believed Billy to be her son.

Billy was trying to fight the yawns overtaking him when Delphi took him back from Steele and cuddled him close to her.

"You're very good with him," Micah said, as she backed away from the crib and watched the heavy-eyed baby wriggle over onto his tummy, his lashes falling on his cheeks.

"I love him."

"A very good thing to do. Every mother should

love her child, don't you think?" Micah waited for her to close the bedroom door. "But I believe you should get him a bigger bed and he should be in a room of his own by now." He preceded her down the stairs.

Delphi bit her lower lip to keep from telling him that Billy had a perfectly good bed in his own bedroom downstairs in the Griggses' apartment. "Ah . . . Mr. Steele . . ."

"Micah. I call you Delphi. Call me Micah."

Delphi inhaled deeply, preparing to argue with him, then she shrugged. It was too small a thing to argue over. "All right. I will call you Micah. Now, Micah, will you please leave?"

They reached the foyer, but instead of leaving, Micah took hold of her arm and led her back into the living room.

Damn female, he thought in exasperation. She didn't even want to hear what he had to say! "Now look, Delphi, I'll leave. But I would like to have your promise that you will let me see you now and then—dinner, dancing . . ."

"I don't think that's a very good idea."

"Look, can we talk about this over dinner? Say tomorrow evening? You've heard rumors about me and I admit some might be tr—"

"I'm sure lots are true," she snapped.

"Now, you're the one who's interrupting."

"Sorry. . . ." Delphi looked at the clock above the mantel. Sam and Nora would be back in less than an hour, she guessed. She didn't want the uncomfortable situation that would arise if Micah were there and started asking questions. "I hate to be rude, but I must ask you to go now," she said softly, but firmly.

Micah stared her up and down like a CAT scan inching over her body. "Very well," he said at last.

"We won't talk tonight. Say you'll go out with me tomorrow evening, and I'll leave."

Delphi's eyes slid from the man to the clock and back again. She could go out with him once, then never see him again. "All right. . . . If you leave now, I'll go out with you tomorrow evening."

"I have the distinct feeling that you are trying to hide something from me, Delphi." He shrugged, his slashing smile going over her like a laser. "And the day will come when there will be no more hidden things between us. Believe that!" The door slammed behind him and Delphi sagged against its oaken frame.

"Dear heaven, that man is Dracula incarnate," she whispered to herself. She wandered into the living room and touched the familiar objects there, trying to soothe herself with the ordinary, the usual. She'd felt as though Micah wished to draw the very blood from her body. She shivered, then dropped down to sit on the sofa and stare sightlessly at the floor.

Delphi ran for the crosstown bus that would take her to Wolf's studio, where she was doing a commercial for a new diet soft drink. Delphi grimaced at the thought of all the chemicals that would be in the product she would be persuading people to taste. "A job's a job," she muttered as she clung to the strap on the bus.

"I ain't givin' up my seat, no matter what you say under your breath, lady. . . ." A bleary-eyed, wrinkled-suited man, close to retirement age, looked up at her from his seat. "First come, first served."

"Fine," Delphi replied mechanically. Her thoughts focused on the question of when—if ever—she would have the freedom to pick and choose her accounts like other higher paid and more popular models.

"And don't think that sad look gets to me. It doesn't. I have a daughter who looks just like that when she asks for the car. She totaled it last Thursday. . . ." The man looked at a bemused Delphi with distaste.

"Yah, I know what ya mean," a man standing next to Delphi chimed in. He, too, glared at her.

She was relieved to get off the bus at the next stop and walk the short distance to the studio. After the photo sessions, she would have to go down to the television studio and practice her lines before the commercial was shot later in the day.

"Delphi, love," Wolf greeted her, not looking away from his precious camera, "there won't be time for more than a few shots today. It seems you're wanted downtown as soon as possible."

"Why didn't someone call me earlier? It's a damn long bus trip here."

The photographer shrugged. "Who can know the mind of the power that is?" he mumbled, gesturing to her to go into the changing room.

The next forty-five minutes were flat-out speed and maximum number of changes.

"I am not a zephyr . . ." Delphi panted as she was pulling on the jumper top of an outfit used in the commercial. "I can't change faster than the speed of light, either."

"Sorry, lamb," Wolf murmured many times in the minutes that followed. Then the session was finished. "See you next week," Wolf said as he turned back to his cameras.

"Simon Legree," Delphi muttered, pushing at the tendrils of hair escaping from the coil on the top of her head.

She could feel the slight beading of moisture on her upper lip as she hurried from the studio, shrugging into her coat in the elevator, then running across the small lobby to the outside. The chill December wind cooled her flushed face as she searched the crowded street for an empty taxi. The cold penetrated her skin as she huddled in her unbuttoned coat. "Damn, I'll bet I'll have to catch another bus!" she exclaimed under her breath. Her anger simmered at the faceless authority that had sent her on a wild goose chase. She could have skipped the work at Wolf's altogether until the following week if—

"Delphi, stop shivering and get in." Micah Steele looked at her through the windshield of his hunter green Ferrari, sunglasses making his eyes opaque and unreadable as he held open the passenger door.

"You don't live around here . . . do you?" Delphi said with a smile before sinking back into the warmth of the front seat.

"No, but I wasn't fast enough to catch you before you left your apartment this morning, so I called Wolf and told him to make your session brief because I would be picking you up."

"You! You're the one who is jerking me around like a puppet on a string! Why didn't Wolf tell me it was you?"

"Because I told him not to." Micah looked over at her, smiled, gunned the motor of the car, then swerved into traffic.

"Of course," Delphi grated out. "Mr. Steele, I went to a great deal of trouble to get to Wolf's studio this morning and—"

"I know. You'll be compensated. I just wanted you nearby when lunchtime rolled around so that we could eat together."

"I'm having dinner with you," Delphi pointed out.

Micah glanced at her again, his mouth feeling dry because this woman had great appeal for him. She was untidy, her lip gloss smeared, he recognized, but she was even more beautiful to him than she had been at the Battersons' party.

"Mr. Steele, are you listening to me?"

"Yes. We're having lunch together now and dinner together this evening." Micah weaved through the traffic, not seeming to notice the drivers who shook fists at him and shouted.

"Eeek." Delphi closed her eyes. "You are a crazy driver."

"No. I'm not. I respect cars and the damage they can do, but I think it's fruitless to line up behind a stalled car and toot the horn. I would rather go around. It's easier on my temperament."

"Not on mine." Delphi looked out of one eye only until he swooped down into an underground garage beneath the television studio and parked.

"Open your eyes, darling. You'll get used to my driving after a time, but if you don't, then you can drive us wherever we go."

"Me? Drive a Ferrari? Don't be ridiculous." Delphi felt again that funny tingle all over her skin when he took hold of her arm. The man should be registered with the police as a dangerous weapon, she thought.

"Now where are you?" There was irritation in his voice. "You have the damnedest habit of—"

"If you mean thinking, Mr. Steele—"

"I mean mind wandering, Delphi. And stop calling me Mr. Steele. Micah is the name." He pulled her close to his side as they stood in the elevator. "Micah is my name . . ." he repeated, his face coming down to hers, his black panther eyes, flecked with brown and gold, seeming to pin her to his side like a butterfly to a board. His lips just teased hers, but he could feel his heart jump as though he'd had shock therapy. It had been a long time since a woman had reached him like this one had. He mulled this over and rapidly cast it away like an uncomfortable shoe. She was a woman who interested him. That was all. . . . .

The kiss deepened and when he felt her stiffen as though to pull back, he yanked her hard against him, the velvet texture of her mouth making his pulse race.

He lifted his head almost at the same time the elevator door opened, but he didn't unlock his arm from around her. It pleased him that there was a glazed look to her eyes. The vague disquiet he felt deep within himself, he tried to ignore.

Delphi jerked free of him, moving forward out of the elevator like a toy soldier, not able to look the receptionist in the eye when she gave her name.

It needn't have worried her. The woman looked past her and directly at Micah Steele.

"Good morning, Mr. Steele. Mr. Fergus has Mr. Tyler with him—"

"Thank you, Gladys." He looked down at Delphi, then kissed her on the mouth. "I'm sorry I can't spend the rest of the morning with you, sweetheart, but I'll be tied up in meetings all morning." He kissed her nose. "I'll pick you up at noon." He whirled away from her and strode through double doors to the inner sanctum of the executive suites of the studio.

"Ah, Miss Reed, you're wanted in Studio C." The receptionist called Gladys studied her as though she were a newly discovered microbe.

"Thank you." Delphi moved down a long corridor, aware that people spoke to her, but she couldn't answer them. She alternated between fury and horror at what had just passed between Micah and herself. She wanted to kill him for embarrassing her like that . . . but she also wanted to know why her pulse and heartbeat were leaping through her skin.

Two

When they broke for lunch, Micah was there to take her hand, kiss the palm, and smile at her in front of the producer, director, makeup person, wardrobe mistress, and all the sundry helpers and cameramen in the studio.

"Don't try to brand me as one of your 'collectibles,' Micah!" Delphi was seething as she tried to free her hand without success.

"You are one of a kind to be sure, darling. Couldn't fit any mold. Come on, we're having omelets for lunch at Figaroa's." Micah towed her behind him to the elevator, barely acknowledging the presence of another soul in the group of familiar people around them.

At the end of the day, Micah was there to drive her home.

"Don't be silly," Delphi protested. "I always catch a bus. It takes me right to my corner and you'll want—" She was about to say that he would want to go home and dress when she realized he had changed. He wore a silk evening suit in midnight blue, and a pale blue silk shirt that appeared to be handmade, with tiny pleats down the front.

His smile crinkled the skin at the corners of his eyes. "I keep clothes in all my offices, and Steele Industries is just down the block from the television studio."

"Oh."

"I didn't want to waste any part of the evening with you, so I'll be taking you home and waiting while you change."

"I don't think I have any crackers and cheese," Delphi mumbled irrelevantly.

"What?" Micah's head slewed her way for a moment then he barked with laughter. "Sweet girl, I'll survive . . . just thinking of you undressing upstairs . . . walking to the shower without your clothes . . " his voice sank lower and lower, the huskiness deepening, "the water coursing down your—"

"Stop it, Micah!" Delphi's voice was a mere croak, her breathing constricted.

"Yes. I'd better stop." He shook his head, then laid the palm of his hand on her knee. She was one potent lady. Lord, his libido was out of control and they hadn't even had a drink together. It amused and annoyed him that he couldn't remember ever feeling his control slipping like this with a woman . . . until Delphi.

Micah parked in front of her brownstone, then came around to help her out of the Ferrari. "This is a very attractive building."

"It is now," Delphi replied, inserting her key into the lock of the front door.

"Is that you Del?" Sam came out of the door of his apartment into the foyer of the building, shared by the Griggses and Delphi. He went over to her and kissed her cheek as he always did. "I think you started something, love . . . oh, excuse me, I didn't know you had company." Sam inclined his head at a frowning Micah.

"Micah Steele . . . Sam Griggs." Delphi introduced them. "What were you saying about me starting something?"

At that moment there was a shout from Nora, then Billy came through the doorway like a miniature steamroller. He was grinning and gurgling at Delphi, roaring "Duhwy . . . Duhwy . . ."

"That's what I mean!" Sam sighed as he watched Del lean down and scoop the wriggling bundle into her arms, kissing his cheek and muttering love words into his neck.

Nora was right behind her son, out of breath and a little frazzled as she was introduced to Micah. "Billy heard you come in. Right away he decided he should be going upstairs with you." Nora shook her head. "You're too much of a mother to him, Del. In fact I'm sure some days he thinks you *are* his mommy."

Delphi could feel Micah stiffen at her side.

"He isn't yours, Delphi?" The soft words fired into her back like darts into a board.

Sam and Nora laughed.

Delphi summoned up a weak chortle.

Billy gurgled.

Micah released phosphorus into the atmosphere.

Bitch, Micah thought. She deliberately let me think the boy was hers. He lifted his hand to her waist, letting his fingers knead the soft flesh. "Darling, hadn't you better give Billy back to his . . . mother? You have to get dressed for the evening."

"No . . . I . . ." Delphi tried to move free of his hand.

"Oh, sure, Del, you go ahead. Come to Daddy, buster. It's time for your story."

"Sto-wy." Billy punched his father with his chubby fist.

The short ascent in the small elevator to her third-floor apartment took seconds, but the atmosphere was so explosive that it seemed to Delphi like an eternity.

"Why?"

Delphi jumped at the bulletlike word from Micah and when the doors opened into her foyer, hurtled across the small space and hastily put her key into the safety lock.

Micah pushed open the door, then took her arm, turned her to face him and stared into her eyes.

She felt her mouth open, and close before any sound came. "I . . . I just didn't feel like explaining anything to you."

"And you thought having a child might be a deterrent to my coming to see you?"

"Maybe."

They stared at each other for long moments.

Micah was angry and puzzled. He wasn't used to women wanting to get rid of him. It rankled. "Get dressed, Delphi." He released his hold on her arms and watched her cross the room and ascend the curving staircase. Her tall figure swayed rhythmically, causing a familiar restless heat in his lower body.

Once in her room, Delphi wanted to run to the bathroom, lock the door, and stay there for two months. Instead, she went to the old rosewood armoire she and Sam had found in the attic of the house and which she used as an extra closet. She threw open the double doors.

"If I had a shroud, I'd wear it," she muttered as she pulled a salmon silk suit from its hanger and placed it on her bed. From the dresser she selected stockings in a flesh color with salmon seams down the back of each leg. Her silk briefs were the gift of a hosiery company for which she modeled and had tiny garters embellished with lace to suspend the stockings. Her bra and slip were of the same pale silk, light and wispy as cobwebs.

She hurried through a shower, but took the time to shampoo her hair, which was sticky with spray and had been teased, yanked, and pulled into different do's throughout her modeling sessions. It hurt her head if she didn't shampoo it clean after a day like that.

When she was putting her earrings in her pierced ears, she surveyed herself. The salmon suit with the clotted-cream-colored ascot slashed in Daliesque ruby, turquoise, and gold was set off by the dangling circles of gold in her ears. She had brushed her hair into a coil at the neck; the style was severe and allowed her high cheekbones and the smooth curve of her jaw to show prominently. Her eyes looked huge and jewellike as she touched blush to the bone line high on her face. Marty was right, she thought, makeup could change one's image.

She stood back from the mirror, glanced at her thin gold dress watch given to her by her parents on her graduation from college and realized she had kept the great Micah Steele waiting for forty-five minutes. She gave a last tug at the jacket of the suit, stared at her bone-leather slings with the four-inch heels that she rarely wore since it made her an even six feet two and much too tall for most men. Then she grabbed the clutch purse that matched her shoes and left the room.

Micah heard Delphi's bedroom door open and close and rose to watch her cross the balcony to come down the stairs. He sucked in his breath. She really was a beauty! What other woman with that fall of red hair, now swept back so severely, would dare to wear that pinkish color? He shook his head and watched her until she disappeared in the stairwell. He hurried to meet her. She would be his, he vowed, no matter what damned bitchy things she did to get out of it.

When he met her at the bottom of the stairs, he forced Delphi to pause on the second from the last step. He had to look up a fraction into her eyes. "Lovely lady, you are tall. I'm six five myself." He placed his hands at her waist and lifted her off the last step to stand close to him. He kissed her hair, his nostrils flaring at the clean lovely body scent of her, traced with the elusive fragrance of Joy perfume. He felt a weird rage that another man would be giving her such a personal gift. "Who buys you such an expensive scent?"

"Sponsors give me gifts." Delphi raised her eyes to his and forgot to tell him to stop questioning her about everything. "And I'm well paid. What makes you jump to the conclusion that a man has to supply me with something expensive?"

"Sorry, darling." He loved the fiery glint in her eyes. "Shall we go?" He helped her put on a short black velvet evening jacket lined in white silk. "I'd like to buy you an ermine. It would be glorious with your hair."

"Don't bother. I wouldn't wear it. I made this jacket and I like it."

Micah could feel a grin stretching across his face. "You're so damned prickly!" he said as he preceded her out of the apartment and punched the button to open the door of the small elevator.

Delphi's chin jutted out. "I'm sure you don't like independent women, Mr. Steele, but I'm—"

"There you go prejudging me again." He held the elevator door open for her and followed her when she went to say good night to the Griggses.

She was silent when he led her out the front door

and over to his car; and she was silent during the short trip across Manhattan.

They ate at Papillon and, though Delphi tried not to, she couldn't help rubber-necking a little. A host of celebrities marched through the restaurant, most of them pausing to speak to Micah and stare at Delphi. Micah didn't introduce her to anyone.

"If I had known that you would be looking at everyone but me, I wouldn't have brought you here." Micah brooded, irked that she could have such an effect on him, detesting the truculence he could hear in his own voice.

When her smile broke through like the sun and laughter bubbled out of her, his whole being did a back flip into delight.

"You sound like Billy," Delphi commented, then watched the play of emotions across his face: warmth replaced coldness, amusement replaced irritation. "I promise to be good," she went on, "if you eat all your vegetables." Impishly she put her fork into her salad and held it up to his mouth. She almost fell off her chair when the powerful Micah Steele opened his mouth and took the food from her fork.

"Thank you, darling. According to the customs of my mother's people, the Anapoloses, who are Greek, engaged couples feed each other at table. Can I consider myself engaged to you, my love?"

"Never," Delphi croaked. "I wouldn't be caught dead with a three-time loser!" She gasped. His face took on a saffron hue, his eyes becoming a black hell.

"So . . ." His sibilant hiss coiled around her like a stinging lariat. "It offends you that I have been married three times."

"It's none of my business." She pushed the words through wooden lips.

"True, but I will tell you all about my past anyway, *agape mou.* My first wife, Nessa, died after the birth of our daughter, our second child. She had a cancer. Please!" Micah held up his hand. "No platitudes, I—" He stopped to glare up at a waiter who dared approach. The man melted away. "I then married Ellen Trine, the actress. Divorced, no progeny. Next I wed Mavis Durney, the sculptress. Divorced, no progeny. And, yes, I thought I loved all of them." He shrugged. "At least I thought I approximated the emotion. I have vowed never to marry again. . . ."

"Good idea." Delphi swallowed hard, her eyes sliding away from him.

There was silence for a time as a waiter served their entrees, lobster for Micah, *truite en couleur* for Delphi.

The silence continued even after they were alone again.

"I wasn't prying into your life. . . ." Delphi sipped some water when a piece of trout burned her mouth.

"I want you to know about me. I have no intention of marrying again, that's true, but I do want to live with you. Will you insist on marriage?"

"No . . . what I mean is, I'm *not* going to live with—"

"Have you been married, Delphi?"

She flicked an irritated glance at him. "You are always interrupting me."

"Sorry. I'll do better. Have you been married?"

She looked into his eyes, chewed her trout, and readied herself to tell him to jump off a bridge. "I almost married once. I carried his child . . . saw him in bed with another woman, miscarried the child a month later and never saw him again. He lives in Los Angeles where I was living at the time." She sipped her wine and wondered why she had told Micah all that. And why did she feel a sense of freedom rush through her, the burden of losing her child lifting from her heart for the first time since it had happened five years before in the hospital in California.

"That was rough, love." Micah leaned across the table and covered her clenched hand with his, loosening her death grip on her knife.

Delphi felt her eyes fill and shook her head. "I'm over it . . . truly I am. . . ."

"You must have loved him very much," Micah grated out.

"No." Delphi lowered her voice, looking around her. "No." She looked back at Micah, then down at the hand covering hers. "I hated losing the child. That was my grief." She raised her eyes to his. "That's why I will never marry, nor have children."

Micah felt shaken to his shoes by the rawness of emotion revealed by her expression. "Then let me take care of you, watch over you." He knew he wanted to do that more than anything in the world.

"I . . . I . . ." Delphi felt caught by those black eyes, fascinated by the yellow and brown flecks there, knowing that in another life he had prowled the jungle.

The waiter placed dessert menus in front of them.

Delphi blinked, looked down at their linked hands for a moment and sighed.

He was ready to kill the waiter, who must have been new, and demanded the check. Micah was too aware of his own worth not to know that he was a preferred customer wherever he went and shouldn't have been disturbed. "Let's go. . . ." He fired some words at the waiter, slashed his name across the check, and surged to his feet, rounding the table to help Delphi from her seat. He shepherded her quickly to the door.

"Are you Greek *and* English?" Delphi huddled in her velvet wrap as they walked the one block to Le Club to dance.

"Darling, I told you." Micah put his arm around her shoulders and held her close to his side. "My name is German but my father Americanized it. My mother's family is Greek with a little English in there somewhere. I'm a mongrel."

"But you attended school in England or lived there for a short time," Delphi insisted. "There's a flavor of British accent to your speech."

"I attended Oxford for three years." He shrugged. "I went to a great many schools—some I was flung out of, bodily."

Delphi laughed, picturing the boy, Micah Steele, thrown out of school. "Not Oxford?" She was still chuckling as they hurried through the door of Le Club.

"No. By the time I went there I was a little more settled. My critics will tell you that I haven't settled yet, of course."

"I agree with them," Delphi dared to say, looking at the tall Lucifer at her side.

"After we've been together for a while, you might change your opinion." He grinned. "Your face is very red."

"A gentleman wouldn't take notice of such a thing." Delphi pursed her lips, not wanting to laugh at him. He had a big enough head already, she mused, without realizing that she thought him a delightful companion.

"Good evening, Mr. Steele." A soignée woman in a silver lamé sheath came up to them. "We're delighted to see you and your companion. It's a bit crowded this evening, but there's room."

Delphi wondered if anyone had ever told Micah Steele there wasn't room for him . . . anywhere.

They were seated and promptly got up to dance.

It delighted Delphi that like so many large men, Micah was a very rhythmic dancer.

They sat down at times to sip at their drinks, but more often than not they stayed at the table only moments, returning to the floor to tango, to gyrate to rock and roll, even to disco.

"Darling, I love holding you," Micah crooned to her.

And I love having you hold me, Delphi moaned to herself, but it's damn dangerous.

When he took her home, he came up in the elevator with her, even though Delphi assured him it wasn't necessary.

When he took her key from her and opened the door, he stood watching her as she walked across the small foyer to the living room. "Stop it, my sweet. I have no intention of forcing you, but you must have felt the power between us. I want to see you tomorrow for breakfast, for lunch, for dinner—"

"I'll get fat," Delphi cut in. She hiccupped a laugh.

"Delphi, I'm not leaving until you promise to see me again."

He had promised he wouldn't push her if she would just have dinner with him. She had just had it, but the argument died before it was fully formed in her head.

"Delphi?"

"Yes."

"Yes, what?" Micah whispered.

"Yes. I agree that we should see each other again."

Micah felt as though his chest had swelled to twice its size as they stood almost a room apart staring at one another. She was like an explosion inside of him, tearing into him. Heat built throughout his body. He wanted to sweep her up and make love to her right there in the middle of the beautiful Oriental rug in the living room. He swallowed and lifted his hands, then let them fall. "I want to kiss you, but I can wait." He turned abruptly and left her apartment.

Delphi buckled into a chair, staring in front of her, seeing nothing. "Tomorrow I'll change my mind. I won't want to see him again. I'll ignore him. . . ."

But her dreams were filled with Micah Steele . . . laughing, frowning, smiling, dancing, holding her. . . . She woke the next morning with a dry mouth, a headache, and the feeling that she had run the marathon, not slept for seven hours.

She had showered and was standing in her briefs and bra selecting a blouse and trousers to wear when the phone rang. "Yes?"

"Good morning, darling, has your doorbell rung yet?" Micah's voice came through the wire like hot honey.

"What? Doorbell? No . . . I . . . wait. It just rang." She held the receiver close to her ear and stared at the bedroom door. "I have to put a robe on."

"Don't you dare answer that door unless you are dressed," Micah commanded.

"Ah, no, I won't. Just a minute," she called. "I have to hang up."

"No, don't hang up. Just answer the door but put your robe on first."

Delphi put down the phone and reached for the terry-cloth robe she used in the mornings. Then she dashed down the stairs, calling to whomever had rung the bell again that she was coming.

She opened the door on the chain and saw Sam there, holding a silver basket with yellow roses in it.

She slipped off the chain and took the basket, thanking Sam for bringing the roses up to her.

Delphi ran to the kitchen phone and picked up

the receiver. "The flowers! They're beautiful!" she said, out of breath.

"So are you, my love. See you for lunch."

Every day was like that all week long. Delphi saw Micah for breakfast, lunch, and dinner. When she wasn't with him, she itched to see him and was delighted when he called her three and four times a day.

Micah was very open in his feelings, both to Delphi and anyone else around them. He not only showered her with flowers and phone calls, but also was there every day to drive her to work and to pick her up in the evening. More often than not, he would come right up to the studio to get her, kissing her hello and embracing her.

It was reported in one of the gossip rags that Micah Steele had a new love interest and her name was Delphi Reed.

When Micah took her out on Friday evening, he didn't tell her where they were going until they were parked in the underground garage of his apartment building. "I want you to see it." His eyes were like black velvet as they went over her in the elevator taking them to his penthouse.

Dinner was a crab-meat dish with vegetables that Micah took from the oven himself. "I have a manservant who lives in an apartment in this building."

"You own the building," Delphi stated.

"Yes." He smiled at her. "You get to toss the salad."

After they had eaten Micah took her on a tour of the two-story apartment.

"My personal quarters are on the second floor, but down here"—he led her down a corridor past the fully equipped chrome and oak kitchen—"are the guest rooms and a study or sitting room for visitors."

Delphi looked into the two bedrooms, each with a bath, that shared the common study. "These bedrooms are larger than mine."

"Are they, sweetheart?" Micah kissed her hair. "Usually my children, Dory and Paul, use the rooms when they're in town, which isn't often." They strolled back into the huge living room carpeted in white. The furniture in the square conversation pit in front of the fireplace sported furry black and brown upholstery. The rest of the living room was raised from the pit by one step and that, too, had modern decor in blacks, browns, and blues.

Delphi looked around her, then at the dining area that was up three steps at the far end of the room. Floor-to-ceiling windows wrapped around dining and living areas so that the large terrace was accessible to either space.

Micah flipped a switch, lighting the terrace and swimming pool. "It's regulation size and heated, love, so if you like to work out by swimming . . ." His mouth grazed her cheek.

"I do like to swim," she murmured and looked up into his eyes. "I haven't said I would live with you. . . ."

"I want to make love to you, Delphi . . . not just once, but many times, for many days, for many years. I want you with me." He held her in a loose embrace. "What do you want, Del?"

She inhaled a shuddering breath, not able to look away from him. "I want you to make love to me . . . for days and . . ." The words died in her throat as Micah swept her into his arms, his mouth meeting hers, like metal drawn to a magnet.

Their lips moved and locked together, enjoying, giving, exciting each other.

Micah broke from her, his heart pounding, his

head reeling, his hands clenching and unclenching on her. "Darling, I love you. . . ."

Delphi put her fingers over his mouth. "No 'forever' declarations, Micah. My feelings for you are just as explosive, but we both know these emotions are fleeting things, not long-lasting. I want us both to go into this with the understanding that this is not a lasting commitment . . . that when either of us wants out, we go."

Micah couldn't get his breath. He felt as though someone had shoved a steel pole into his midsection. Her words echoed those of his he'd said many times . . . and genuinely believed. He'd always believed that a relationship based on an understanding of its impermanence was the best sort of liaison between a man and a woman. But those ideas coming from Delphi hurt like hell! He pulled her close to him and smothered the ache in his gut with her body. "Whatever you want. I'll have my lawyer draw up a contract tomorrow. It will contain everything we both want and it will all be nice and legal." He looked down at her and felt the jolt those silver-green eyes had been giving him, the jolt that had become so familiar to him. "When will you come to live with me?"

"When do you want me?" Delphi choked out.

"God. Now, darling. Right now." There was a sheen of tears in her eyes that pulled at his heart. His pulse picked up speed at the green velvet softness to her eyes. He needed her! "Now, darling," he breathed, then leaned down to lift her slowly into his arms. "Do you know how long I've wanted to do that? Hold you? Carry you?" He groaned when she lifted her arms around his neck and nuzzled her face there.

"How long?" Delphi swallowed, tightening her hold on him. She had wrestled with this decision all last night in her solitary bed, all the while wishing Micah was with her. "How long have you wanted to hold me?" she muttered, recalling the long night she had had.

By the time pink dawn light had sliced at the darkness, she'd decided to live with Micah. Though she might have him for only a short time . . . though she knew she would have hosts of hollow years yearning for him when they parted, still she decided to take the brief happiness he offered her, rather than never have Micah in her life at all. In three short days of seeing him constantly, he had brought sun into her life; in four days he had taught her to appreciate the perfumes of life, not just those of the flowers that he sent her constantly, but the smells of fabric, ink, bodies . . . and Micah himself who was so male, so strong, his odor limy and astringent, clean and masculine. By the end of six days she knew that she would live with him when he asked her, which she sensed would be soon. All the banshees, ghosts, and goblins that she could conjure up against living with Micah blew away like smoke when she thought of the man himself. "I need him," she had told herself in the night. "I want the happiness that he brings me . . . and though there will be the loss of him one day, I want the time with him now." She had rolled over, punched her pillow, and gone to sleep until her alarm woke her at seven-thirty.

Now as he carried her up the stairs to his bedroom, whispering love words in her ear, all she felt was a raging anticipation to love and be loved by this man.

He lowered her to her feet, letting her body slide down his body. He knew a sudden, unaccustomed anxiety that she wouldn't like his room. He had designed it himself and he liked it, but he fully intended to change everything if Delphi didn't approve.

Delphi looked around the expansive, cream-colored room, accented with oak. An American Indian rug covered the floor and she knew it must have cost a fortune because it was almost room-sized. The geometric patterns in reds, blues, and creams warmed and invited. The monstrous bed covered in cream silk with blue and red throw pillows was a delight. "It's lovely. I like it very much." She looked up at him, feeling drowsy, yet charged. "So, this is the passion pit that everyone talks of."

"Wrong." Micah lifted her hand and sucked on her baby finger. "The passion pit is an apartment downtown. No woman has lived with me here . . . ever."

"Not even your first wife?" Del whispered.

"I didn't own it when she was alive."

"Oh."

"Do you want to keep things as they are? Or change them? Whatever you want is fine with me." He noticed how his hand trembled when he ran his finger down her cheek. Damn. He never recalled any other woman having such power over him . . . yet he relished it. He fiercely wanted her to hold him, to dig her nails into him, clutch him . . . and never let him go.

"I like it just the way it is. Perhaps I could bring a few things of mine. . . ." She stared up at him, not able to resist putting her hand to his hair, the crispness of it making her whole body tingle.

"Darling, bring anything you want. I'll move all your furniture over here—"

"No, no." Delphi laughed and rested her cheek on his chest, loving the thud of his heart vibrating on her skin. "Just a few things . . ." She let her fingers crawl down his back until they locked at his waist. "But I thought we came up here for a more elemental reason than discussing furniture." She chuckled when he swept her up in his arms again, and delighted at the convulsive tightening of his hands when she blew in his ear. "I hope you're feeling sexy."

"That's stating the obvious." Micah stood her on her feet near the bed and began unbuttoning the bodice of her dress that was a sea-green silk shot with threads of gold. "I like this dress, so I'm going to try to be careful . . . but dammit, woman, if you keep looking at me like that, this lovely garment will get torn."

"Naughty," Delphi said breathily. She nipped his chin, her own hands working the tiny gold studs in his shirt front. "The next time we are having a stay-at-home, tell me. Then I'll wear a robe . . . only."

"Yes, do that. Now that you are moving in with me, darling, I think we will be having a great many stay-at-homes."

"True." Delphi felt the silk slide down her body and made no effort to catch it. Since she wore no bra she was garbed only in slip, stockings, and briefs. When Micah continued to stare at her, she gently tapped him on the lips with the nail of her index finger. "There's more, you know . . . clothes to remove, I mean."

"I know. I just like looking at your breasts. They're full and perfect and tilt up." His voice was hoarse. "And your nipples are such a lovely shade of rose." He bent and took one into his mouth, his other arm going around her waist. When he heard the low, keening sound of her satisfaction, his heart leaped in his chest. "Darling, Delphi, sweetheart . . ." he muttered as he pulled back from her again and stripped the rest of the clothes from her body, tossing them away.

He lifted her onto the bed, her body stretched out before him. He pulled at his shirt and yanked the trousers from his body, flinging the clothes away until he was naked as she. When he would have dropped beside her, she sat up, taking his breath away as her flesh quivered in movement. "Where are you going?" he croaked.

"Nowhere. I just thought we might like to get under the cover." She swung her legs to the floor, her back to him as she rolled back the silk cover, carefully.

Micah couldn't take his eyes from her long graceful back. He placed his hand on her buttocks, then his other hand reached around her waist to pull her back to him. "Darling, damn the cover. Can't you feel how ready I am to love you?"

"Yes." She whirled in his arms. "And I am ready to love you." She reached up and pulled his head down to hers, their lips locking together.

Even when they swayed and fell back on the bed, their mouths didn't release their hold on each other.

When they were supine, hip to hip, thigh to thigh, Micah began a slow sensual search of her body.

Delphi could feel the restlessness of his aroused body and how it was inflaming hers.

"I dreamed of this for so many nights, wanting it to be good for you, promising myself that I would go slow, tease you, love you . . . caress you. God, Delphi, I can't go slow with you. I need—"

"I know what you need. I need it too," Delphi crooned to him, feeling a melting sensation in her thighs and calves as passion built between them.

When he penetrated her slowly, he felt her body jerk. He retreated and lifted himself up from her. "Delphi? It isn't the first time for you. It can't be. You've conceived a child."

She shook her head, her hair splaying out on the pillow. "I haven't . . . wanted to make love in a long time."

"How long, angel?"

"Five years." She gasped when he hugged her to him, caressing her with his hands and his mouth.

"Sweetheart! All that time!" His lips traveled down her neck to her breast, his tongue teasing the nipples there, then taking one into his mouth to love it gently.

"Don't hold back, Micah . . . aaah, that makes me feel so funny, fluttery. I want you to love me. . . ."

"I know, I know." He continued to touch her everywhere, his hand following his mouth, in a soft, sensuous rhythm that had her gasping. "God, darling, you are so sweet. I'll want to love you forever. . . ."

"Don't say forever. . . . Oh, Micah, please . . ." The high, helpless sound of her own voice surprised her. Then she forgot everything else but Micah. He entered her world, came through the handleless door that only she could open to her heart and locked himself to her in the quiet violence of sexual love.

Delphi couldn't make a fist. There was tingling feeling all through her, but she couldn't lift her foot, even smiling was an effort, yet she knew that she had never been so alive.

"Open your eyes, sweet one. . . ." Micah blew on her cheek.

"Can't." Delphi giggled, feeling anchored, yet totally free. "Everything is so heavy."

"Eyelids too?"

"Oh yes. Lovely," she burbled, burrowing closer to Micah's chest. "I had no intention of ever letting you close to me." She pulled at the hair on Micah's chest, not opening her eyes. "I was going to be too smart for you . . . never join your harem." Her eyes popped open. "Now here I am . . . and I like it."

"You are not *in* my harem. You *are* my harem."

Micah slid down her body and took hold of her foot, kissing each toe, then the arch, then the ankle. "You are the only woman for me. You are my one-woman seraglio."

"That's nice." Delphi sighed, tugging at his hair so that he would come up to her face to face. "You are the only man in my life."

"Right. It is going to stay that way." Micah punctuated each word with a kiss.

"Can you see into the future?" Delphi tried to smother a yawn with her hand and failed. "Goodness, I'm sleepy. Why do you suppose?" She was puzzled when Micah laughed but she smiled at him anyway. "Lovemaking doesn't make me tired," Delphi informed him as she assumed she knew why he was laughing.

"Doesn't it?" Micah kissed her cheek and cuddled her close to him. "You would hardly be considered an expert on lovemaking, my sweet."

"No, that's true, but I still know it doesn't make me sleepy." Delphi snuggled into the warmth of Micah's chest, smiling when she heard him chuckling.

Sleep came like a handmade quilt, soft, cuddly, warm.

When she woke, she struggled through the veil of sleep, vaguely aware she wasn't in her own bed, but not worried about it.

"I love you," Micah whispered to her, his hand whorling over her bare skin.

"Thank you. I love you, too, even though it is silly for us to be in love. What time is it?"

"Five-thirty."

"In the morning?" Delphi jackknifed to a sitting position, feeling the silken sheet slide down her body. "Lord, I have to get home. I have an early appointment."

"Cancel it. I want to stay in bed today." Micah snapped on the overhead light and looked at her.

Delphi laughed and threw herself onto his chest. "Stop scowling that way. You look like a petulant little boy."

"I feel like a king," Micah assured her. "I may run up to the roof of the building, thump my chest, and give a war cry."

"You'll be arrested." Delphi stopped wriggling when his hands began the sensual insistent probe that told her that the love play was beginning again. "I should go home now." She turned to face him, her hands coming up to cup his face.

"After tomorrow, this will be your home." Micah's words were slurred.

"Not so soon," Delphi gasped. "I have to talk to Sam and Nora . . . and lease my apartment so that I can make my mortgage payments." She could feel him shrug under her hands.

"I have a man who handles my real estate dealings. He'll take care of your place, leasing it, getting your things moved."

"But I still have to talk to Sam and Nora," she said faintly.

"Fine. Take the day off and talk to them . . . but tomorrow you will be living here. I won't be without you one more day."

"Little boy!" Delphi chuckled, then she pushed at him when he tried to enfold her closer. "I have to work. I'm committed to the commercial and Wolf is doing the—"

Micah snorted in irritation to cut her off. "Okay, but have him shoot fast, then you can use the afternoon to talk to the Griggses." He nibbled on her neck. "I want you with me. Don't you want that?"

"Yes. Oh yes, Micah, I do want that," Delphi

sobbed into his neck, her body arching against him, undulating against the hardness of him.

"God, Delphi, you're like velvet . . ."

Words and movements increased until there was a crescendo of love murmurings and caresses. Then as they spiraled higher, their passion mushroomed, exploding around them so that they were alone in a tactile world of delight, sensation building on sensation as each of them strove to give the other the greater satisfaction.

"You are mine, Delphi."

"And you are mine, Micah."

Three

News about them traveled like flash-flood waters
into every corner of Delphi's and Micah's lives, so
that even the man who shined Micah's shoes commented on the gorgeous redhead and gave his
approval to the liaison.

"Darling," Micah said to her one evening as they
prepared to go over to the Griggses' apartment and
play cards. "You couldn't expect that our relationship would be a secret." He grimaced, then stepped
into corded brown slacks, the same warm choco-
late color repeated in the silky corded shirt and
vest.

She floated across the room to him to be enfolded
at once in his arms. "I know . . . and the last six
weeks have been all the happiness in the world to
me. What other people say really doesn't matter,
but tomorrow . . ." She licked her lips and grasped
his shoulders. "Paul and Dory are coming." She
exhaled a shuddering breath. Her voice rose.

"They'll hate me. At eighteen and sixteen, they won't need a reason—"

"Stop that. They'll love you. I've told them all about you." Micah leaned away from her, his hands on her shoulders. "It's true they didn't care too much for my other wives, but Ellen and Mavis didn't like children and I kept Dory and Paul away from them. It worked better that way. With you it will be different. You'll see."

"I hope so," Delphi murmured. Despite his reassurance she had a heavy feeling in her stomach at the thought of meeting his children. She could imagine their animosity.

They went to the Griggses early because Delphi wanted to see Billy before he went to bed.

"You miss the little guy, don't you?" Micah sat in the passenger seat, his hand caressing her leg from knee to thigh.

"Yes. Billy is such a darling." She gasped and pushed at his hand. "Micah Aristotle Steele, stop that. We'll get into a traffic accident. You should have driven."

"No. I like you to drive and you need the practice for when you have your own car . . . and don't say you don't need a car in New York City. By next week you'll have a pale-green Ferrari almost the color of your eyes." Micah couldn't help smiling at the thought. It made him happy to give things to Delphi, not that she let him give her all the things he felt she should have.

What amazed him most was that he did enjoy riding with her. He couldn't remember ever wanting anyone to drive his cars, but it delighted him to watch her hands on the wheel, her right hand shifting the gears.

"Are you picking apart my right turns, darling? Is that why you're so quiet?" Delphi chuckled, happiness bursting out of her. Laughing and smiling had become a common occurrence now. Sometimes she felt as though she would float right through the stratosphere, that space travel was something she had already conquered. She loved Micah, she knew it, but kept silent about commitment. If commitment wasn't a part of their relationship, how could anything between them be broken or separated? She would have a day-to-day heaven with Micah and not worry about the future.

The streets of Manhattan were slushy and cold and there were patches of ice that were a hazard to both drivers and pedestrians.

When she parked the Ferrari in front of the brownstone, she sighed and turned to look at Micah. "How did I do?"

"Wellll, you almost took out two old ladies, one paper vendor—" Micah covered his head as she leaned toward him, buffeting him with her gloves. He loved their horseplay. Just having her touch him at all sent his pulse up two notches. He grabbed her wrists and pulled her close to him. "You know how much I love to wrestle with you, but if we don't get out of this car right now, we won't get to see Nora and Sam, let alone Billy." His tongue flicked out and touched the corner of her mouth. He knew such a surge of masculine power every time he felt her body tremble as it did now.

"Bad man," she crooned to him, then pushed him toward the door. She knew enough to wait for Micah to come around and escort her from the car. It angered him if she didn't wait until he could open the door for her.

Sam and Nora met them when they walked into the foyer; they stamped the snow from their feet and were quickly ushered into the Griggses' warm apartment.

Nora immediately took Delphi's arm and led her up the stairs to Billy's second-floor bedroom.

"Duhwy . . . Duhwy," Billy thundered, jumping up and down in his crib and shaking the sides.

"Yes . . . yes!" Delphi laughed as she swept the chubby boy up into her arms and kissed his clean, sweet-smelling skin.

"Man." Billy pointed to Micah, who stepped forward and held out his arms to the child, who went into them at once.

Delphi could feel a strange tearing sensation in her chest as she watched those big hands hold the child. Micah was so strong . . . but how gentle he was! She shivered, recalling the feel of those long fingers on her own flesh.

When Billy was settled, Delphi and Nora left the bedroom together. Micah and Sam had gone downstairs a few minutes previously.

"Del . . ." Nora stopped her by putting a hand on her arm. "He is not only a gorgeous hunk, he's a nice person too."

Delphi nodded. "He is gentle and kind, but I'm sure his business associates don't see him that way."

"I have never seen you so relaxed, so happy, Del. You were always attractive and stylish, but . . . but now you glow, you're beautiful." Nora put her arm around Delphi's waist.

"I'm happy. He makes me happy." Delphi stopped at the foot of the stairs. "But tomorrow his children are coming to stay for their winter break from school and I'm so nervous."

"Don't be silly, Del. Just treat them like your own." Nora shrugged. "They'll love you."

Delphi could feel her face grimacing as they walked into the living room.

"Let me guess." Micah rose to his feet and came over to Delphi, kissing her lips. "You have been telling Nora how worried you are about having Paul and Dory come tomorrow."

"Right." Nora laughed, then turned to tell Sam what they were talking about. "I told her to treat them like her own."

"Good advice." Micah led Delphi to the card table and seated her.

The evening was fun and since they kept rotating as partners, bridge playing rules were sometimes bent out of shape.

"Men cheat." Nora threw in the last trick, then glared at Micah and Sam. "It was not possible for you to win all those hands unless you cheated. Come on, Del, help me with the coffee."

When they drove home, it was after midnight and Micah drove with Delphi huddled as close to him as she could get. Even with the heater on the night was clear and very cold.

"I like them," Micah said, turning his head a bit so that he could kiss her on the forehead.

"I'm glad. They have been my closest friends since coming to New York—"

"Four and a half years ago," Micah finished, knowing almost as much about Delphi as she did about herself. Many nights they would lie in bed and tell each other anecdotes about themselves. He found those times when they were clasped close to each other after volcanic lovemaking to be a delight. They would exchange confidences, giggling and laughing about the bloopers they had made. He found himself storing up all those things about Delphi, savoring them.

Sometimes, when he was sitting in meetings, his mind would wander to her and he would recall something funny she had told him about herself. Often it was all he could do not to laugh out loud. She was in his blood and flesh now, moving through his whole system as though she were part of him. He shook his head in irritation and amusement at how fanciful he had become. She had made him lyrical, poetical, a new person . . . and he liked himself—no, that wasn't right. What he liked was living with himself now! He enjoyed his solitude, found people more interesting, discovered earth and sky in all the colors of the spectrum.

The next morning Micah had his work cut out for him, trying to calm Delphi. "Darling, stop it. You've rearranged the flowers in that vase three times."

The doorbell rang and Delphi whimpered, trailing after him as though he led her to her own hanging.

"Paul . . . Dory . . ." Micah laughed, then embraced two tall, dark-haired, dark-eyed teenagers, who laughed back at him. The boy punched his father's arm, the girl reached up to muss his hair.

The three were smiling when they turned to face Delphi.

She could feel her face whiten. The smile froze on her mouth, her lips locked, and could get out no words of welcome.

"What have you been saying about us, Dad? She looks scared to death!" The smaller version of Micah walked toward Delphi with one hand outstretched.

Delphi's lips unstuck and she moved forward to take his hand. "You're Paul."

"I'd like to give you a real soul kiss . . ." Paul twinkled at her, the raw charm that would plane itself into the smooth sophistication of his father as he aged manifested itself. "But my father can get uptight about some things."

"You'd better believe it," Micah growled, bringing his daughter forward with his arm around her waist.

"And you're Dory." Delphi swallowed, her insides feeling less feathery.

"Short for Dorinda"—Dory made a moue—"but please don't call me that." Her smile slipped sideways as she looked from her father to Delphi.

Why, she's as nervous as I am! Delphi felt empathy and relief. "I promise never to call you Dorinda, if you don't call me Delphinium. . . ."

Shouts of laughter from the two teenagers made Micah grin broadly at a grimacing Delphi.

"Where's your luggage?" Micah looked behind him with a frown.

"We left it in the outside hall." Paul shrugged. "You know, just in case you wanted to be alone."

"Fool." Micah grabbed his son around the shoulder.

"You're different," Dory said, then turned beetred, rolling her eyes. "Dad will kill me for saying that."

Delphi laughed and gestured for Dory to come with her into the living room. "He won't kill you, if he doesn't know anything about it."

Dory sat down across from Delphi, the coffee table laden with fruit and canapés between them. She at once picked up an Anjou pear and bit into it, sighing. "We have the rottenest wet clay food at school. Sometimes I just die for a piece of fruit." She dabbed at the juice on her lips with a napkin and smiled at Delphi. "What I meant before was . . . well, Dad's other wives . . . I mean ladies, didn't want us around. Ellen was always rehearsing for a part and Mavis was always busy sculpting a masterpiece. . . ." Dory made exaggerated sweeps of her arm in imitation of a great artist. "Not much of her stuff was that good, I didn't think, but she sold most of it . . . thank God." She bit her lip and giggled when Delphi laughed.

Del was delighted with her new "children" and instead of their staying for two days, they stayed for the entire winter break. When they left, Delphi felt a sudden loss, a loneliness.

"What's this? Are those tears I see in your eyes?" Micah came up to her and put his arms around her as she stood in the middle of their bedroom.

"Stupid, isn't it? They are so like you . . . with that quick wit—" She shook her head, laughing. "The two of them almost drove Wolf crazy during a session the other day. He couldn't stop laughing at them, then he took us out for lunch. . . ."

Micah looked down at her shining eyes and felt a wrench. She had loved his children almost at once . . . and they had taken to her. How special she was! "I never expected them to go to your appointments with you."

"Paul loved driving the car." Delphi chuckled. "Dory loved the makeup and the clothes. Wanda Dathrop, the wardrobe mistress at the studio, gave Dory the full treatment one day and I thought I would never be able to get her to wash her face."

"They have never had anyone pay so much attention to them before." His lips quirked upward. "They even called you 'Moms' in front of the Griggses." Micah grinned.

"Sam, the rat, loved it." Delphi reached up to stroke her man's brow. "I must say I didn't mind when they called me that." She leaned back from him a moment. "And weren't they good with Billy?"

"Very . . ." Micah shook his head. "I never thought either one of them would care about a baby."

"Kids are unpredictable."

"Is that right, 'Moms'?"

"That's right." She smiled up at him, her hands linked around his firm waist. "By the way, haven't you forgotten something?'

"What?"

"We're alone in the house. Want me to chase you through the rooms with a whip and a chair?"

"Forget the whip and chair, but"—Micah's eyes deepened to a hot liquid glow—"but chasing after that derriere of yours. . . !"

"I get the picture!" Delphi backed away from him and began unbuttoning her dress.

"Oh, Lord, how awful it is what you do to me, Del. Before you had the first button undone, I was ready." Micah threw his shirt into the corner, not once taking his eyes from her.

"Did I ever tell you about the time I took belly-dancing lessons with a friend?"

"No. I'd love a demonstration." Micah swallowed, his pulse doing the familiar skip it always did when he watched Delphi undress.

She strode to the wall console and pressed the stereo switch, dialing until she had the tape she thought appropriate.

From all corners of the room, sensual rhythm swirled through the air.

Delphi, who found the console an entertainment in itself, pressed another switch to dim the lights to soft pink. Another button caused a portion of the ceiling over the bed to slide back, revealing a mirror. "I still don't believe this was all here when you bought the building."

"I swear!" Micah had his eyes glued to her, as she turned to face him, dressed only in briefs.

Her hair was down and she was barefoot as she looked up at him. Hands steepled over her head, her head and body began a slow sinuous motion. She seemed to take the slow, jungle beat of the music into herself as she gyrated and twisted in front of him.

Micah felt pain. He wanted her so badly, but he forced himself to stay the six or so feet from her, in order to watch her dance. She was the most incredibly sexy woman he had ever known, but there was such an innocence to her, such a chaste goodness. A saintly Circe?

Goosebumps rose on Delphi's skin as she saw Micah's naked body become aroused. She did so love this man. Every pore in her body reached out to him. She loved belonging to him, she thought with a poignant sigh. She would always belong to him, no matter when they parted or how long they were apart. Micah would have her always.

"Darling, Delphi, I have to stop you, my love." Micah was at her side, sweeping her up into his arms and carrying her to the bed.

"Micah," she sighed into his neck, "I was just beginning my routine."

"And I had just reached the end of my control, love." His mouth slipped from hers, down her body, marking each curve and indentation as his own. "Maybe after a hundred years I'll have more control—" He froze, choking off his sentence as he felt her stiffen. Every time he mentioned a span of time they might be together, or any kind of commitment to one another, she went rigid on him. It never failed to anger him, frustrate him, but he didn't show those feelings to her. She was too touchy on the subject.

It hurt her when she felt his body grow taut, but she closed her eyes and held him closer to her. She determined not to put herself through the purgatory of wondering when Micah would tire of her— that was a never-never land that she wouldn't contemplate. She would face it when necessary.

Thought disappeared in the furnace of love they fed with gentle but insistent caresses, kisses that clung to flesh, hands that searched and probed. Legs and thighs rubbed in increasing restlessness, toes cramped and flexed as their bodies reached out for one another, the satisfying culmination reaching deep into their souls and marking them, one for the other. They chased the world away, climbed an unclimbable peak, achieved the success of the world because they held tight to one another.

Delphi felt a languorous dizziness as her breathing became regular again. "It's scary," she murmured, her head on his chest. She loved the feel of his chin rubbing the top of her head.

"What's scary, sweetheart?" He felt so good. It delighted him as always to know that he would fall asleep with Delphi held close to him. He yawned.

"That every time we make love, it's better, more exciting, yet so serene, so . . . so tingly."

"Tingly?" Micah chuckled, his eyes closed. "Crazy lady. You use the strangest words to describe making love . . . but I like your way with words, your way with lots of other things too."

They slept with their arms around each other.

The week after Paul and Dory left, Delphi noticed that she was dizzy once in a while during the day.

"Hey, Del, what's the matter?" Wolf asked her one morning when they were shooting.

"I don't know. I think I'm getting a cold or something. I'm so thirsty and I feel funny."

"Listen, girl, you get to a doctor. You can't take out time for a cold when we have such a big week ahead of us." Wolf argued with her for an hour about seeing a doctor.

Finally she agreed to make an appointment with Sara Templar, her internist.

Sitting in Sara's office the next day after an examination, she watched as the doctor flipped through her folder, making notations, pushing half-glasses up on her nose. "Ah, Sara, it isn't anything more than a cold, is it?"

Sara looked up. "Isn't a cold. I think you're having a reaction to those birth control pills you've been taking. I'd like you to stay off them for a while." Sara smiled at Delphi. The two women had been friends since Del had first gone to her for a checkup when she arrived in New York. It was then that Delphi had told her about losing the baby. "I don't think you'll have too many problems convincing Micah to use something just until we can put you on something else. I'd like to see you in a month or six weeks and we'll check how you're feeling then."

"But you did say that with my tipped uterus, I could have a hard time conceiving anyway?"

Sara shrugged. "Sometimes that is the case, yes, but since you have already been pregnant . . ."

"But I was younger then too."

"True."

On the way home Delphi decided not to mention to Micah about using an alternate contraceptive. He would begin to worry and perhaps insist that she not work for a while. Lord, he was liable to sign her into a hospital. She muttered to herself about Micah's overprotectiveness.

"Wha'cha say, lady?" The cabdriver looked in his rear-view mirror.

"Oh . . . er . . . nothing. Just talking to myself."

"I get all the nuts," the driver said darkly.

She and Micah had a busy schedule during the balance of February and throughout March. It wasn't until April that Delphi went back to visit Sara.

"You look good," Sara told her prior to examining her. "Feeling all right?"

"Wonderful," Delphi assured her. "It must have been the pills. I haven't been dizzy once or felt tired. In fact I seem to have more energy, and I've gained a couple of pounds. Of course I don't want to do much of that."

At the end of the examination, Sara told her to get dressed and meet her in the office.

As Delphi sat down opposite the doctor, Sara smiled at her. "So you decided to go without anything, huh? Well, I think your prayers have been answered."

Delphi could feel her smile wobble. "What do you mean, Sara? What prayers?"

Sara stared at her, her smile pursing into a frown. "Delphi, you're pregnant . . . early, maybe a month or six weeks, but still very much an expectant mother. Didn't you guess?"

"No," Delphi said, through lips as stiff as cardboard. "I haven't been sick. With the last pregnancy, I had morning sickness right away. I knew . . ." Her voice trailed off.

Sara lifted a shoulder. "Pregnancies differ." She shook her head. "I'm sorry, Del. I guess I've given you bad news." She bit her lip. "If this is going to complicate your life, I can give you the name of an abortion clinic. As you know, I don't perform abortions."

Delphi stared at Sara, blinking, until the words sank into her brain. "Abortion? No! No abortion! Kill my baby? Never!" She stood, pacing the small office. "Things will have to change, but I will have this baby." She felt an all-encompassing sadness. It was not Micah who would be leaving her. She would be leaving him. God, it had never occurred to her that she would be the one to leave.

"Delphi? Listen to me. I'm going to give you the name of a friend of mine . . . here in the city."

"Ah . . . no. Do you happen to know anyone . . ." Delphi hadn't thought of her uncle in a long time, but she knew that he still looked after the lake property that had been deeded to her on the death of her father. "Do you happen to know a good obstetrician upstate, say in Rochester or Syracuse?"

Sara nodded. "Yes, I do. I have a friend who is at the Medical Center in Rochester. She's a crackerjack obstetrician by the name of Jill Harmon. I can give you a letter of recommendation." Sara sighed. "You look unhappy, Delphi. Are you running away?"

"Hiding out is a better way to put it." Delphi smiled weakly. "Neither Micah nor I intended to have children or to marry, but I want his child." She stopped pacing and faced the other woman, feeling a wetness on her cheek. "He would want to marry me. He is an honorable man, but he's been married three times, Sara, and none of them was a really happy arrangement. He has a distaste for marriage and I am not going to see what we have between us disintegrate into dust."

"Delphi, listen to me. It's better to talk to him about this—"

Delphi held up her hand, palm outward. "No. Micah and I have already talked through this very subject. We have even signed a contract between us, stating that there would be no children, no marriage, no permanent ties, that if either one wanted out, the other would not stand in the way." Delphi hauled in a painful breath, shaking her head. "Sara, I am the one who is leaving as soon as the opportunity presents itself." She could feel her throat clog. "I can't go until . . . until he's out of town . . . away for a short time. I'll leave him a note, reminding him of our contractual agreement," she faltered, her hands hanging loose at her sides.

"Delphi, my dear." Sara rose and came around the desk, pulling the younger woman into an embrace. "Don't do this to yourself."

"Have to . . ." Delphi struggled to hold back the tears. "It sounds silly, I know, but I . . . I promised that we wouldn't have children—and I want this child."

"Delphi, Micah isn't a monster. You even said he's kind and gentle." Sara shook her. She was filled with an impotent anger that people in love should hide themselves from one another.

"He is, he is. But please, Sara. I'll think about this. If I change my mind about telling him, I'll call you." She backed away from her doctor, swiping at her eyes with one hand. "But . . . but you mustn't tell . . ."

Sara waved her hand impatiently. "Of course, I'm not going to tell him, but I still feel this is stupid."

That evening when Micah came home, he was tired. "Darling, let's just have something on a tray, listen to music." He hugged her to him, feeling a sense of well-being as he held her, some of the frustrations of the day melting away.

"Did you have a rough time with Elfridge?" Delphi rubbed her cheek against his chest.

"Yes. How did you know?" He sighed. She was so easy to tell things to, hash out the day with, unwind.

She leaned back from him, one hand coming up to stroke the slight growth of beard on his chin. "You said you were having lunch with him, and you mentioned that he was a bastard in the conference room." She smiled up at him.

Micah barked a laugh and kissed her cheek. "He is."

"Micah, darling . . ." She rubbed his jaw again. "I hate to remind you, but we can't stay home and have a tray tonight. The Arbuthnot party is tonight and you told me your secretary sent an affirmative answer to the invitation, so I marked it on our calendar."

"Dammit!" He buried his face in her hair. "I forgot."

"I could call and cancel if you like."

Micah looked down at her, feeling his being expand with happiness. The Arbuthnot party was at the Helmsley Palace Hotel and there would be scores of celebrities there. He knew that Delphi loved to watch celebrities, yet the serene look in her eye told him she would give up the evening at a nod from him and feel no loss.

He could feel a frown crossing his face, as he reached down to lift her chin higher. "Darling, aren't you feeling up to par? You look a little pale. Have you been working too hard?"

Delphi wanted to laugh as she watched the bulldog expression come over his face, but she was prepared. They had lived together long enough for her to know that Micah Steele noticed things that escaped the scrutiny of others. "No, I haven't been working too hard. I just walked home this evening and I'm feeling a little tired."

"Damn you, Del," Micah scolded her mildly, putting his hand behind her knees and swinging her up into his arms. "Did you leave your car home again and take a bus? I think I'll beat you this evening," he said into her hair.

"Before or after we take a nap together?"

"Before." He chuckled, shaking his head.

Later, when she was feeling a sweet lassitude after their lovemaking and subsequent nap, she stood in front of the rack in the walk-in closet. She was covered by a silky wraparound and stared at the numerous outfits. "It looks like a branch of Charine's," she muttered, shaking her head.

"What did you say, darling?" Micah walked to the door of the closet from their bathroom. He rubbed his hair with a towel, another towel cinched around his waist. "You probably need some new spring things. I'll call Charine and set up an appointment for us."

Torn between horror and amusement, Delphi whirled around. "You will do no such thing. I will never wear half the things in this closet."

Micah frowned at her. "Many of them will be out of style and, besides, you told me that if I sent a check to World Hunger each time you purchased clothes it would be all right."

"But, darling, I didn't mean it would be all right for me to go on shopping binges every month." Delphi walked toward him, her hands spread wide in a request for understanding.

"You never let me give you furs; you only have one car; you would only take one ring from me; you sent back your pearls . . ." An angry, hurt expression chased across his face before he thrust out his jaw like a sulking little boy.

Delphi laughed, reaching up to catch him around the neck with both hands. "You would give me the world if I didn't stop you."

"I would love to give you the world." Micah's hands were at her waist and he lifted her off the ground. "You make me so happy," he whispered against her mouth.

"Micah, my darling!" Delphi sobbed, pressing her mouth to his, her tongue reaching for his. "I love you, love you," she mumbled against his mouth.

An alarm rang within Micah. "Delphi, sweetheart, what's wrong?"

"Nothing. Sometimes it gets to me. We have so much, don't we?"

"Yes, we do." His eyes searched hers, probing, hunting for an answer. What wasn't she telling him? An elusive, empty feeling assailed him. He had often had this nagging sensation when things were not going right with a business deal. He stared down at her, wary and uncertain.

Delphi looked up at him, seeing the play of emotions in his expression. Micah was too sharp. "Help me choose one of these old rags to wear," she demanded, turning her back to him. "My goodness, what junk. This closet is filled with silks and woolens. They will all have to go." She waved dramatically and heard him chuckle from a spot just behind her.

"Stop baiting me, woman." He stepped closer and inhaled the clean scent of her hair, feeling relaxed, but not able to smother completely the worry that snaked through his system. He shook his head to clear it and lifted one hand from her body to pull a silver chiffon silk from the closet. It was a wisp of a dress, layered in a diagonal swath and looked as though it were composed of large, flat ruffles.

Delphi looked up at him over her shoulder, shaking her head. "You love silky, filmy clothes."

"On you, I do. You're so beautiful. Like Aphrodite, your slender body floats . . ." He waved his hand, then looked down at her and grinned. "You had better get dressed quickly, or we'll be back in bed again."

"So? Who's complaining?" Delphi turned in his arms, clutching him for a moment, her face pressed to his chest. "I love you, darling."

"And I love you," Micah said slowly, one hand coming up to lift her chin.

"I'm late . . . I'm late . . . for a very important date . . ." Delphi parroted the White Rabbit in *Alice's Adventures in Wonderland.* Then she broke free of him and went to rummage through drawer after drawer of silken undies until she came up with pale smoke-colored briefs. The dress was lined so no slip would be required and its off one shoulder bias style wouldn't allow for a bra.

Delphi could feel Micah's eyes on her as she pulled on the soft gray nylons she hooked to the garters of her briefs. It delighted her that Micah always wanted to watch her dress, and it never ceased to amaze her that she didn't feel the least embarrassment either when he dressed and undressed in front of her. They were totally comfortable with one another.

"You have great legs, darling, and silver hose do show them to advantage." Micah frowned for a moment. "Arbuthnot's construction men better be on their best behavior."

"Tell me about the people who will be there." Delphi stood, smoothing down her dress, then slipping into silver kid slings with three-inch heels. She decided to wear a cashmere jacket threaded with silver to ward off the chill of the April evening.

"Wait, angel. Wear these with it." Micah grinned down at her as he opened a jewel box. Moonstone drop earrings and a thin band of moonstones on a gold bracelet winked up at her. "Not expensive, but I still sent a check to World Hunger."

Delphi shook her head, laughing. "How many of these little surprise boxes do you have hidden away?" She was taken aback when she saw his face turn a deep red. She tried not to laugh but couldn't help herself. "Micah Aristotle Steele!"

"Not many. When I see something I like . . ." He shrugged, then scowled. "You took the pearls back."

"Darling . . ." Delphi reached for him. "I promise I will never do that again. I can see how much you enjoy buying things for me."

"So much."

"But you still mustn't do this all the time."

"Very well. Did you really say you wouldn't return anything I bought you in the future?"

"Yes," Delphi answered warily.

Micah turned away and went toward their dressing room.

She followed him, watching while he went to the wall safe where they kept their valuables and twirled the knob.

He reached for a black suede case with the Cartier name on it. "Here, my darling, these are yours."

Delphi took the case, opened it and gasped. "The pearls!"

"Yes, my love, the pearls. They were a very special purchase. The earrings and the ring are flawless natural pearls, their luminescence like your skin. They belong to you."

Delphi looked up and caught the flash of vulnerability in his expression and nodded. "They are mine . . . and I thank you, my dearest." She looked up again. "Would you like me to wear them tonight instead of the moonstones?"

Four

The Arbuthnot gathering was like a cattle drive with the hands in tuxedos, rather than jeans, Delphi thought, as she looked around.

"You would rather be home, sitting on our own couch, listening to music while I fondle your body," Micah leaned down and whispered in her ear.

"Micah." Delphi laughed, looking up at him and nodding. "Stop reading my mind."

"Micah, my boy, how are you?" A bluff, roly-poly man with a rose-hued face stepped in front of them.

"Bernard." Micah shook the proffered hand, his left hand urging Delphi forward. "Darling, this is Bernard Deal of Deal Associates. Bernard, this is Delphi Reed."

"How do. And this is my wife Wilma . . ." He gestured toward a thin woman of medium height who wore a very expensive outfit that did nothing for her. "Wilma, you remember Micah. And this is Delfee, his friend."

"I am relieved," Wilma Deal said. "For a moment I thought you might have trodden the matrimonial boards again, Micah. And marriage isn't for you, is it?" she asked rhetorically while looking pointedly at Delphi.

Perhaps even a year ago Micah would have laughed and agreed with the acerbic Wilma, but now he could feel a slow fire building in the core of him. The bitch! The twice-spawned bitch of a bitch! Where the hell did she get off—

Sensing his mounting anger, Delphi squeezed his arm hard to bring his attention on her. "Darling, didn't you say we had to meet someone?"

"What?" Micah tore his gaze from Wilma. He looked down into silver-green eyes glinting with amusement. "Yes. We said we were going to meet someone. Bernard. Ah, Velma . . ."

Wilma Deal blinked three times. "My name is Wilma!"

Micah walked away and didn't look back.

Delphi skipped every other step so that she could keep up with him. "Whoa, cowboy."

"I should have tossed her through a window," Micah grated out through clenched teeth.

Delphi slid to a stop at his side as he gestured for a barman to fix a drink for them. "Darling, it was unkind of you to pretend that you had forgotten her name."

"It was either that or punch Bernard in the nose. I like him too much to do that to him." He gazed down at her. "You are so very beautiful with your curls all piled on top of your head. Your hair flashes so red in the light and that dress makes your eyes appear to be more silvery than ever. You're perfection and I damn well won't let anyone make innuendos, or snide remarks."

"I love you, silly man. Nothing anyone says changes that." Delphi took the glass of chilled Riesling from his hand and sipped the sharp wine.

A man almost as tall as Micah and wider slapped him on the shoulder. "Glad you could make it." He turned at once to Delphi and picked up her hand. "Trust you, Micah, to bring the most beautiful girl in New York to our party. Introduce us."

Micah put his arm around Delphi and moved her back so that her hand was freed. "Sweetheart, this is Larry Arbuthnot, president and chief executive officer of Arbuthnot Associates."

"We do a great deal of construction work for your . . . for Micah both here in the States and in the Far East and Africa, Miss Reed."

"Yes, Micah and I have talked about the Outreach program in Niger and Nigeria," Delphi answered, going on to discuss the advantages of building medical centers and learning centers in strategic areas. She put Arbuthnot at ease and drew him out on the problems associated with projects in which the people progressed on their own, taught by their own, adhering to their own customs.

Micah inserted leading statements that advanced Delphi's observations. He felt swollen with pride as she talked and rebutted with grace. It didn't surprise him when some of the other investors stepped closer and began talking and questioning. Micah studied her. She wasn't just intelligent, but intuitive, as well. She had a photographic memory and she was so compassionate that it almost hurt to hear her speak.

"No wonder you can't take your eyes from her, Micah," Arbuthnot said. "She is not only intelligent, but also one of the most beautiful women I have ever seen. Isn't she on television?"

"Yes. She does commercials." As Arbuthnot had

observed, Micah didn't take his eyes from Delphi's face.

"And no wonder you haven't been visible at any of the watering holes lately."

"I wouldn't be here if my secretary hadn't rsvp'd 'yes' on your invitation," Micah said none too graciously.

Arbuthnot shouted with laughter. "That's right. You never do respond to these things. You just show up . . . or not, whatever suits you."

"Right."

"Micah, listen, have you got a minute? I want to show you some of the plans I roughed out on the plane."

Micah hesitated, scowling, not wanting to leave Delphi, centered as she was in that den of wolves. He nodded once to Arbuthnot then elbowed his way to Delphi's side. "Darling, I have to talk to Larry. I promise I won't be more than fifteen minutes." He leaned down and kissed her full on the mouth, then cast a narrow-eyed look over the assembled group of men.

"I think Micah Steele wants to decapitate us," a bald-headed gentleman by the name of Resson observed.

Delphi smiled, then turned to the man on her left. "What you said about failure of self-help programs is valid, but . . ."

Delphi felt as though she had been put through a wringer by the time Micah rejoined her. When that familiar arm slid around her waist, she leaned back against Micah's muscled chest, sighing with relief and delight. Micah was her love and her security. Her body jerked as though she had been stabbed as she contemplated for a moment what it would be like without him.

"What is it, angel? Do you have a pain?" he

crooned, cuddling her close to his side. "I felt a spasm course through your body."

"Nothing. It was nothing. I was just thinking about going home and making love."

Her laugh sent a frisson of panic up his spine. Something was ringing false. Delphi never lied to him, he was sure of that, but there was definitely something she was keeping from him. He knew her too well to miss the negative vibrations her body sent to his.

"Sounds wonderful," he murmured into her hair, as he led her into dinner in the huge dining room.

When he seated her, he reached down to kiss her neck and felt the taut cords under his lips. There was something cooking. She was as tense as a drop wire. Well, my darling, he mused, whatever it is, we will handle it together. He put it out of his mind and strove to entertain his lady while they ate.

"Miller, isn't it true, that during the strike one of your management men ran a wire for a phone down a grand piano leg in a fancy penthouse?" Micah leaned around Delphi to question the man on her left.

Miller Graves rolled his eyes. "Heavens, yes. Then the old harridan who owned the piano threatened to call the President of the United States if we didn't fix her Steinway."

Delphi laughed helplessly, making the others at the round table for ten insist on hearing the joke. When they did, they also had many stories to add about construction job bloopers, telecommunications mistakes that all companies dealing with the public must face. "I hadn't realized how extensively your company is into civil engineering and communications. Here I only thought you were a computer man when I first met you," Delphi managed to whisper when there was a lull in the conversation and they were alone.

"Steele Associates is into many things, dearest. Some day if you're interested, you might like to try the business world and come and work for our company." Micah smiled when her mouth dropped open.

"You *wouldn't* hire me." Delphi shook her head.

Micah nodded. "Like a shot. I might even make you my assistant. You are so bright, so quick to learn, so eager . . . and so lovely to look at. But of course that could be the one drawback." He kissed her nose. "That's the only time I'm glad you're working. When I get that terrible urge to see you, which I do many times each day, I can fight it if I know you're out shooting somewhere with Wolf or one of the other photographers."

"Darling, I love you," Delphi said simply.

"We have to go home now." Micah groaned in frustration.

"We'll have one dance."

They rose from the table and tried to move toward the dance floor, but each step they took was impeded. Someone was there to speak to Micah and be introduced to Delphi.

She could feel the avid curiosity of some of the people, but it didn't bother her. She felt too secure with Micah to feel uneasy about what others thought of her.

They enjoyed dancing together and though they didn't do as much of it in public as they did in their own living room, Delphi closed her eyes in delight as Micah whirled her around the floor. "Isn't this lovely?" She was slightly out of breath from the fast tune when the musicians changed tempo.

Someone tapped Micah on the shoulder and it startled him so that he released Delphi and watched, narrow-eyed, as she was swished away by Larry Arbuthnot.

Later when they were in the car and heading home, the silence was a bit heavy.

"Darling? Micah? What is it?"

"Did you enjoy dancing with Larry?"

It took Delphi a minute to realize to what he was referring. She chuckled. "Are you jealous?"

"Yes. And don't laugh, Del. I hated the feeling. I was ready to flatten a man who has been my close friend for more than fifteen years. I may do it yet." He punched the words out his mouth as though they were hot rivets.

Delphi crooned, leaning against his arm, one finger twirling in his hair. "You know you have no need to be jealous. There couldn't be another man for me." How her insides wrenched at the truth of her words.

"I know that, but I couldn't stop that feeling of jealousy. I don't want anyone putting his arm around you, holding you." He hit the steering wheel with his hand. "I have never in my life felt that way about anyone, and I damn well can't help it." He looked at her in amused irritation when she laughed. "Stop that."

"All right, but just wait until we get home and I get you into the hot tub and . . . well, just you wait. What a punishment you're going to get!"

"Damn you, Delphi, look what you've done." He lifted her hand over onto his lap, pressing it into the bulge there.

"I think I know just the cure for your problem, sir."

"So do I." Micah sent the car slewing around a corner, accelerating up a grade and flashing through a light blinking yellow.

"Micah, slow down. You'll be arrested."

"I don't want that. By the way, love, I have to go

out of town for two days. Arbuthnot wants me to look at the scale model for that treatment complex we're building in Africa." Micah threw a quick grin her way. "He wanted me to stay for a week, but I couldn't keep away from you that long. I'll probably be calling you every fifteen minutes."

Not so soon! Delphi screamed in her mind. She wanted longer with him. "Ah . . . darling, don't bother calling me. I'll arrange for Wolf to do the location shooting while you're gone and that way we . . . we won't have two separations." She tried to cough away the hoarseness in her voice.

"Are you getting a cold?" He was getting that feeling again. She was withdrawing from him. Damn. What was it? "Delphi, I have a funny feeling that there's something you should be telling me . . . and haven't."

"You should have been a detective." She scrambled around in her mind for a red herring. Damn the man for being so sharp! "I've been offered a contract with Lisson Industries to be one of their cosmetics models, but the job would take me to California." It was true about the contract, but she had already told her agent that she wouldn't accept it.

"If you take it, it will mean moving my office to California." Micah shrugged. "No big deal, really, we have a branch office out there. So I'll just switch places with someone, but it will be tough not seeing Paul and Dory as often."

"True." Delphi leaped at the opening he had given her. "That's what I'll tell Kenny . . . that it would be too inconvenient—"

"Good!" He swung the car down the ramp to the underground garage, not looking at her, but sensing she seemed relieved. If that was the problem, it certainly was solved quickly enough, Micah mused, going around the car to open her door.

Then he forgot what he was going to say when she swung her legs toward him and reached up one slim hand. "God, I could eat you . . . plain." Slight pressure brought her to her feet and into his arms. "Would you mind if I feasted on you, darling?"

"Feel free." She clutched him round the neck, pushing her face into his skin. "Hurry, Micah. I want to love you."

"Sweetheart, that's what I want." He clamped her to his side as they hurried toward the elevator. Micah inserted his key, noticing that his hand shook a bit. What an effect Delphi had on him. She had the equipment and ammunition to destroy him. His blood pumped as he took her from the elevator into the apartment, and up the stairs into their room.

Their lovemaking, always satisfying to both of them, was volcanic and almost out of control. They took each other again and again, skin glued to skin, breast to breast, mouths in loving search up and down their bodies.

"Micah, Micah, I will always love you," Delphi whispered brokenly into his neck as he lifted himself over her and plunged deep, the hardness of him piercing her with love and a gentle fierceness that had her gasping and arching against him in explosive fulfillment.

Delphi woke in the night and thought that she was alone. For one frightful moment, she believed she had already lost Micah. She turned in a frenzy of agony and passion to throw herself against his back and hug him to her.

"Wha—" Micah surfaced from sleep alert and aware that Delphi was clinging to him and that she was distressed. "Angel . . . ?" He turned over on his back and lifted her onto his chest. "What's wrong? Aren't you feeling well?" He caressed her silky back, his fingers finding each vertabra, then

sliding downward to pat and rub the downy softness of her backside. "Tell me."

"I want you to love me again," she whispered, her
body in restless massage on his.

It delighted him so much that she wanted to
make love that he could feel excitement and building passion sear his inner being. He pulled her
fully up his body so that when she looked down on
him, her curling hair curtained both of them. He
smothered that alarm ringing again in the back of
his brain when he saw the feverish glitter in her
green eyes.

"We should do this more often, my sweet," he
purred, her breath coming into his, his hands
kneading her velvet backside. "I've been thinking
that Steele Associates should try to market a fabric
that would imitate the softness of your skin, my
love. It would make velvet obsolete."

"Nice man," Delphi responded, her teeth nipping
at his chin and neck, her hands running over his
skin.

Each of them seemed to hold back, as though the
lovemaking had to be savored, stretched, reveled
in, by Micah and Delphi.

They fell asleep with their arms around each
other, their faces pressed close.

"You are my only love," Micah muttered and like
a stroke of lightning that knowledge erupted in his
brain just as his eyes were closing in sleep. His last
thought was serene delight. He, Micah Aristotle
Steele, had done the impossible. He had discovered
love. Any man could go to the moon, penetrate the
ionosphere, flirt with the constellations, but he
had done more. He had built a universe of his own.
He could feel a smile curve his lips even as he
drifted into sleep.

Delphi cuddled to him, like a child trying to
return to the womb. He was her life force, her

blood, her happiness. When she left him, existence would be arid. A life in the desert was her future.

She fought to stay awake, knowing that as soon as Micah made his two-day trip she would be gone. She planned each moment. She would write three letters . . . no four. It would be necessary to write her agent and tell him she was leaving the area. Then she would write to Paul and Dory. She loved them and that's what she would tell them.

Sleep came with the dawn. It would be a clear and lovely day.

Micah had a phone call at breakfast and when he was finished with his very terse conversation, he looked up at Delphi and grimaced. "That was Larry, darling. He says he's cleared it with the plant in Wisconsin so we can fly out this morning."

"Will you be flying yourself?" Delphi tried to smile.

Micah chuckled. "No, I'll have Buzz fly us out, so take that 'I'm trying to be brave' smile off your face."

Delphi exhaled in relief and shrugged. "I trust your skill as a pilot. You know that. It's just that sometimes you fly by yourself, and I hate it."

"I know, sweetheart. That's why I'm letting Buzz pilot the Lear jet. Larry and I will work in the back." He rose from the table, throwing down his damask napkin, then coming around the table to lean over her. "I'll miss you, precious. This will be our first separation and I'm not looking forward to it."

"Neither am I," Delphi whispered, reaching up to him, loving it when he lifted her out of the chair and embraced her.

In forty-five minutes he was gone with one briefcase that included two shirts and two changes of underwear. If he needed another suit, there was always a spare on the plane, not to mention the sportswear kept fresh there.

Delphi sat and looked around the oval morning room, which was a small room off the kitchen where she and Micah ate most of their breakfasts. It faced east to catch all the morning sun. The furniture was rosewood and mahogany that she and Micah had bought at estate sales. On the floor was a pale green Oriental rug with cream and pink accents that made the dark-hued furniture seem to glow with a richer patina because of its colors. "I will never sit in here again," she said out loud in a dazed fashion.

When the housekeeper poked her head around the doorway and asked if she would like anything else, Delphi shook her head mutely, rose, and left the room.

She wrote the letters to Ken, Paul, and Dory, called her uncle in Seneca Falls, then packed the few things she would take with her. In another two months she would need maternity clothes, so she left most of her things where they were. She fingered through the jewel case Micah had presented to her and decided that she would take the pearls and the emerald ring that he had given her. The rest she left.

Everything was done. She knew that as she rubbed her hands up and down the jeans she had donned for packing. There could be no more stalling. She called Wolf and said that she wouldn't be in that afternoon. Then she went to her desk in the private sitting room she and Micah had shared adjacent to their bedroom.

Many times she tried to tell him that she loved him, but somehow the words seemed so milksop, meaningless.

She was sitting at her desk, staring at yet another fresh piece of stationery with her initials scrolled on the top of the fine vellum paper in palest green, when she happened to look up at a book of poetry that she and Micah liked very much. She reached up to the shelf above her desk and lifted down the slim volume that they had enjoyed and turned to a particular favorite. As she read it out loud, the book open on the desk, she began to copy the poem called "Colors" by Yevgeny Yevtushenko.

> When your face
> appeared over my crumpled life
> at first I understood
> only the poverty of what I have.
> Then its particular light
> on woods, on rivers, on the sea,
> became my beginning in the colored world
> in which I had not yet had my beginning.
> I am so frightened, I am so frightened
> of the unexpected sunrise finishing,
> of revelations
> and tears and the excitement finishing.
> I don't fight it, my love is this fear,
> I nourish it who can nourish nothing,
> love's slipshod watchman.
> Fear hems me in,
> I am conscious that these minutes are short
> and that the colors in my eyes will vanish
> when your face sets.

The pen shook in her hand as she reread the poet's words. Then she began writing again, saying out loud the words of *adio*, as the Greeks would put it. "My darling, you are and have always been 'the unexpected sunrise' in my life. I did not know that such a person could exist for another. I had not even known, until I met you, that my life was one-dimensional, that my vision was narrow, that all color was missing from my life. You gave that to me, Micah, my dearest love. The kaleidoscope was mine, the color wheel of living was my own because you loved me. I will cherish that, hug it to me when we are parted. You are my one and only love . . . and in my heart, you have always been my husband, my spouse, my lover, my partner, my rib, my joints, arms and legs . . . all of me. I will be afraid now. Life will have so many gray corners, so many muddy days. Good-bye and thank you for loving me. Delphi."

She left the letters on the dressing table where he would see them. She picked up her one suitcase and her purse, and left.

The plane ride to Rochester Municipal Airport only took an hour, but she felt she wanted to go to Rochester rather than to the closer Syracuse so that she could make an appointment with the obstetrician, Jill Harmon, recommended by Sara.

She decided to rent a car and drive herself into Rochester proper, sign into a hotel, then call the doctor. She was lucky enough to get a cancellation for the next day. Tired, she lay full-length on the double bed in the hotel room and went to sleep.

When she woke, it was dark outside. After showering and changing, she had a meal in the lobby restaurant, then went back to her room to read for a short time. Micah appeared where the printed words should have been. "My darling . . . please . . . please, don't haunt me," she begged in a whisper.

The next day, she asked directions to the Medical Center and drove out in the rented car.

Jill Harmon was younger than Sara, but there were streaks of gray in her blond hair, and though she wasn't as tall as Delphi, she had a slender athlete's build. "You're in fine condition, Delphi, but I think you should be on vitamin therapy."

"Ah . . . Dr. Harmon, I will be staying in Seneca

Falls and driving in for my visits. I wonder if I might have all afternoon appointments."

"Of course." Jill frowned at her. "It might be tough on you in the cold weather, driving this far . . ."

"It'll be fine."

The next day Delphi drove east on the New York Thruway to exit 41 to Waterloo, New York, the exit that would take her to her destination. She had decided not to go to her uncle's house, but call him from her hotel room.

The Gould Hotel in Seneca Falls, New York where she'd made a reservation looked different from the way it had to her as a child. It looked smaller. Before she took her luggage from the trunk, she walked around the building to the marker on the corner that told of Susan B. Anthony's first speech in defense of Woman's Suffrage. She walked back into the building, went up to the small registration desk in the compact lobby, looked around her at the etched glass on the doors leading into the bar, the old-fashioned elevator with the Otis sign so prominent on the brass fittings and the old-fashioned metal collapsing door as you stepped into the lift. One of the dining rooms was already opening for the dinner hours. Delphi's rumbling stomach told her that it had been too long since she had eaten the sliced peaches on whole grain cereal, orange juice, and coffee with cream . . . and taken her vitamins.

"Hello. My name is Delphi Reed. I have a reservation."

"Ah . . . let's see . . ." The man was probably not much older than Delphi. He introduced himself as Flynn, the manager. He looked up at her. "Would you be Delphinium Reed?"

"Yes, my Uncle Wilmore . . ."

"Wilmore Reed is your uncle? Know him well. We

have a nice suite for you, Miss Reed." He came around the desk, then directed a pained look at her luggage. "We would have taken that out of the car for you, Miss Reed."

"Did you say I have a suite? I only wanted a room . . ."

He shrugged, both hands open to her. "Sorry. We had a suite left."

Delphi didn't want to waste the money, but was too weary and hungry to protest at the moment, so she nodded weakly.

The suite was very attractive, in the corner of the building with a medium-sized sitting room and bedroom, and a good-sized bath and shower. Delphi loved the high ceiling and the long windows looking out on the street.

She showered and changed into a skirt and blouse, noting that it was hard to zip up the skirt. She'd be in maternity clothes very soon.

She took a deep breath and dialed her uncle's number.

"Hello. Hello, I say. Who is it?" Aunt Jane's tart voice came over the phone.

"Ah . . . Aunt Jane. It's Delphi . . . Delphi Reed."

"Well, Delphinium . . . and where are you calling from? New York, I suppose. I have been trying to get your uncle to sell that place of your father's on the lake. We could use the money."

"But it's mine . . ." Delphi sputtered. "Dad left it to me, with a sum of money going to Uncle Will to take care of it for me."

"Isn't enough. Inflation. If we get a seller for it, we'll keep our share of the money and send you yours. Now, what was it you wanted, Delphinium? I have to get back to my cleaning."

"Nothing. Just tell Uncle Will that I called."

"Foolish waste of money, I calls it." Aunt Jane slammed down the receiver.

Her uncle had asked her not to phone his home when she'd called him from New York. It was no wonder, Delphi thought. She decided then and there she would take a walk around the town and see how much it had changed in the five years since her last visit.

Delphi tried to clear her thoughts as she walked, still she murmured, "My unexpected sunrise is gone . . ."

"Did you say something, dearie?" An elderly woman, dressed in black and walking with a cane, looked at Delphi, then smiled.

"Ah . . . not really. I was just talking to myself." Delphi smiled back at the woman, feeling the warmth of the sun on her back.

The woman nodded, looking up and down Fall Street. "I do that, but my son says I shouldn't. Are you walking along to the drugstore?" The woman lifted her cane and pointed to the RX sign hanging from a low building just up the street.

"Well, yes, I'm walking that way."

"Good. I'd like the company. My name is Cramer, Aurelia Cramer, and I've lived in Seneca Falls all my life. You aren't from here," the crusty Mrs. Cramer stated, then she twinkled up at Delphi. "I'm also eighty-four. I can say what I think."

Delphi laughed out loud, feeling a touch of lightness as she inhaled the clean air and basked in the sunshine. "No, I'm not from here. I'm just visiting. My uncle, Wilmore Reed, lives on Bayard Street."

"It's nice weather. What did you say, dear? Wilmore Reed? I know him well. He was friends with my brother Barton before he died. Married to that prune Jane Jessup. Can't abide the woman, but Wilmore is a sweet man, henpecked, but sweet. . . ."

Delphi meandered into the store with Mrs. Cramer, then walked her down State Street to her large Victorian home before retracing her steps to the Gould Hotel at the corner of State and Fall streets.

That night her Uncle Wilmore called. "I'm sorry, my dear. Jane told me what she said to you. She had no right. She doesn't know it, but I've used the money your father left for the care of the cottage. It's in good shape for you. I even rented it a few times, but now I only rent it to people I know are going to be as fussy as I am." Uncle Wilmore rushed his words, not talking above a whisper. "Aunt Jane is out in the garden now. How would it be if I came to visit you this evening?"

"Fine." Delphi felt a rush of pity for her uncle because he shared his life with such a domineering woman.

It was smoky dark when her uncle walked into the small lobby of the Gould.

"Uncle Wilmore, here I am." Delphi stepped out of the dimly lit bar across from the dining room, hesitated a moment, then went to embrace the thin, small-statured man who blinked myopically at her. Tears rushed to her eyes as she felt the frailness of him. "Uncle . . ."

"Delphi, darling girl." He clutched her for a moment, then leaned back to gaze at her. "You're unhappy, child."

They talked for a long time, seated at a tiny table in the bar, and since they were the only occupants of the small room, there was a relaxed tenor to their conversation.

"I'm sorry Jane talked to you the way she did. . . ." His jaw tightened. "You needn't worry, child. She has no authority whatsoever to sell your property . . . and she damn well is going to learn that the house she loves so much is mine, coming to me from my father. . . ."

"No . . . no, don't disturb the peace of your home for me, Uncle Wilmore."

"Peace! There has never been peace in my home. . . ." There was soft bitterness in his tone.

"Thank you for all you've done for me, Uncle Wilmore."

He patted her hand. "Give me another day to straighten up the place, then you can move in. . . ." He coughed. "Child, you're pale . . . and more than unhappy, I think. Any way that I can help you, I will." He gave her a watery smile. "You were always the child that I wanted for my own, Delphi, and I love you. Please believe that even though I haven't been able to keep in touch much these last five years."

They parted on a very warm note, with her uncle promising to pick her up in the morning.

That night, Delphi slept with only sweet dreams of Micah. When she woke her cheeks were damp. She scrubbed at them with an angry hand. She had to learn to live without that man and not mope around. He'd made her happy, he'd given her a child. That was a great deal more than most people had in a lifetime. She got out of bed and stretched, marveling that she had none of the queasiness and lassitude that she had felt with her first pregnancy.

She showered, then dressed in jeans and T-shirt with a cotton flannel shirt knotted at her waist. She stuffed a ditty bag with bathing suit, creams, and brown soap in case she encountered poison ivy.

When the phone rang, she lifted the receiver on the first ring.

"Delphi . . ." Her uncle's voice sounded stiff. "I will be around to pick you up in fifteen minutes."

"I need that car," Delphi could hear her aunt state in the background, her voice like a pile driver.

"I told your aunt you were in town. We've had

words," Wilmore said, his tone indicating severe strain.

"Uncle, I have a car. Let me pick you up."

There was a silence. "All right, child. Do you remember the house?"

"Yes." Delphi hung up the phone, feeling guilty and recalling what Mrs. Cramer said about her uncle being henpecked.

She gathered her things together, checked around the room and was about to leave when there was a knock at the door. She opened it and sucked in a painful breath as she looked up into the Luciferlike face of a very rumpled Micah Aristotle Steele.

"Damn you, Delphi," he hissed.

Five

"No," she whispered. Her first flashing thought was how cruel to see him again. How could she leave him twice?

"Yes. Where is he?" Micah pushed open the door, then strode past her, fists clenched. "Did you think you could protect him? Why didn't you talk this over with me?"

"Would you have listened?" She pushed the words through wooden lips, still stunned to see him, watching him shove into the bathroom, then into the bedroom, then back to the sitting room.

"Yes. I would have listened . . . then I would have killed him."

"Killed who?" Delphi tried to rally as he paced up and down the room, darting angry looks at her.

"Where is this man you ran away with? When the hell did you meet him? How dare you leave me?" He punctuated each question by pounding his fist into his palm. "The closet!" he snarled, then whirled again to go back into the bedroom.

Delphi snatched up her ditty bag and went out into the hall, opening the cage of the old-fashioned elevator and stepping in and pressing the button for the basement. She would go out the Rathskeller door to the parking lot.

Looking behind her at every step she smiled weakly at the attendants cleaning the Rathskeller for the entertainment that evening and slipped out the door.

She didn't take a deep breath until she was in her rented Skylark and pulling out of the parking lot. How had he found her so fast? How did he get here so quickly? He still had another day in Wisconsin. Her mind was on automatic pilot as she drove across the bridge over the Seneca River and toward Bayard Street. She couldn't concentrate on her direction because thoughts of Micah whirled through her head.

She stopped the car when she saw her uncle on the porch. He came down the steps, her Aunt Jane standing with arms folded, glaring at the car.

Wilmore reached the end of the walk and opened the gate. It squeaked.

"Get that oiled, Wilmore," Jane said in a high voice.

Uncle Wilmore took two more steps toward the car, halted, and turned. "Oil it yourself," he told the openmouthed woman. "And don't forget that house is mine. So, if you want to live there, stop being so bossy."

A man next door lifted his head from the garden he was weeding. "About time you told her off," he muttered at Wilmore, then went back to his weeding.

Her uncle got into the car, grinning at Delphi. "Taken too much from that woman. Got to be a

habit, but I won't let her get to you. Decided that."
He looked straight ahead out the windshield, his
chin up. "Let's go, girl. Don't dawdle."

Delphi chuckled and drove out of the town
toward Route 89, which would take them down the
lake to Oak Beach Road where the old summer
home was located on a spit of land that reached out
into Cayuga Lake. It was almost isolated from its
neighbors by the three hundred feet of frontage.

Delphi hadn't seen the property for five years
and she felt a nostalgic wrench as they drove down
the winding Route 89 along the beautiful west side
of the forty-two-mile-long lake.

"Uncle, I hope you haven't been working too hard
on the place. You shouldn't—" She happened to
glance up into her rear-view mirror and saw a
black Mercedes following her. Automatically her
foot trounced the accelerator.

"Easy, girl. This is a dangerous highway. You're
going too fast," Uncle Wilmore said mildly. "What
ails you?"

"Ah . . . nothing," Delphi answered, throwing a
quick glance into her side mirror. There were
many people who drove high-powered, fast cars in
addition to Micah . . . and besides his sedan was a
Rolls-Royce not a Mercedes, she told herself, trying
to shake the icy feeling crawling up her spine.

When they had gone fifteen miles, they turned
down a road marked with a piece of oak bark.
Burned into the bark were the words OAK BEACH ROAD.

When the black car followed along behind, she
gulped and felt all the blood in her body race down
to her toes.

"Slow up, Delphi. The driveway is the next one."
Uncle Wilmore sighed. "Lake looks crystal blue
today."

"Yes. It does," Delphi responded like an automa-
ton, her eyes flicking once more to the rear-view

mirror as the black Mercedes swung into the driveway behind her. It followed the short distance to the small barn that was the only building visible from the road, and parked behind her car. "Oh, God," Delphi moaned.

"What is it, child? Did you forget something?"

Delphi looked once more into the rear-view mirror at the black-haired, black-visaged man who got out and slammed the driver's door, then stalked toward them. She flinched. "Uncle Wilmore, listen to me—"

The passenger door was whipped open and a bare, well-muscled arm, sprinkled with black hair, reached in and grabbed Wilmore by the shoulder, almost pulling him from the car.

Delphi threw herself across her uncle screaming at Micah. "Stop that. Don't you do that to my uncle!"

Wilmore's mouth was wide open, his head back against Micah's arm as he looked upward. "Who might this be, Delphinium?" he whispered.

"A fool . . . a . . . a madman," she sputtered, trying to pry Micah's hands from her uncle's shoulder. "Stop that, Micah. What's wrong with you?"

"Then you get out of that damned car and explain why you ran out on me again."

"I owe you no explanations!" Delphi fumed as she got out of the car and faced him over the roof.

"You damn well do, Delphinium Reed." He spat each word at her like a missile.

"Get back from that car and let my uncle out, Micah," she demanded, feeling war erupt inside her. She and Micah had had more than one argument in their time together and some of them had been fiery, but never did Delphi want to fight with him as much as she did today. It would be her only defense against him! How dare he come back into

her life and force her to part with him again! She
could toss him into the lake!

Micah backed away from the car, his eyes still on
her, as Wilmore stepped from the auto. Micah
dwarfed her uncle, but Micah hardly noticed. He
could strangle her for walking out on him. It took
all his self-control not to leap over that car and paddle her backside. He felt threatened, violated, used
. . . and bereft. How dare she do that to him?
"Whatever the hell you're doing, Delphi, you are
not going to get away with it!" he vowed in dooms-
day tones.

"We're going to clean out the inside of the
house," Wilmore Reed explained in a mild voice.

"Huh?" Micah looked down at the smaller man
blankly.

"How'd do." Wilmore pushed out his hand,
blinking up at Micah through his rimless glasses.

"Oh. You're Delphi's uncle. How do you do?"
Micah took the outstretched hand, then shot an
evil glance at Delphi again. "Don't think you can
hide the man from me, Del. You can't."

Her uncle turned around to look at Delphi,
favoring the hand that Micah had shaken. "You
hiding a man, Delphinium?"

"Uncle Wilmore," she gasped. "Do not listen to
this . . . this airhead—"

"Airhead, am I!" Micah roared, making Wilmore
Reed blink several times and take a step back
against the car. "Who the hell did you think you
were fooling? I called you—"

"I told you not to call," she pointed out in a sulky
voice, irritated beyond measure that he had
destroyed her good plan.

"I know you damn well did," he bellowed back,
making a kingfisher rise from the beach, squawk-
ing at the intrusion. "Trying to fool me." His voice
dropped to a spitting whisper. "Where is he?"

"Yes. Where is he, Delphinium?" Uncle Wilmore twinkled at his sputtering niece. He turned back to Micah. "Would you mind if we continued this conversation after I've shown my niece around the grounds of The Embers?"

"The Embers?" Micah cast a wary glance at the fulminating Delphi, then looked carefully around. "This place is called The Embers?"

"Right, first time." Wilmore beamed at him. "Want to come along?"

"I don't want him." Delphi's voice crackled.

Micah stared at her for an electric moment, then he nodded.

"Fine." Wilmore nodded once, then cocked his head at Delphi. "Coming, child?"

"Yes, but I don't like it." Chin up she sailed around the freshly painted cream-colored barn with the shiny black sliding doors and along the path to the house that sat on a fan-shaped knoll looking out over the lake. Stands of pine and maple and poplar screened out the summer homes on either side of the small peninsula that jutted into the stony strewn bottom of the lake.

"It's a nice piece of land." Micah A. Steele, entrepreneur and industrialist, spoke, forgetting his war with Delphi for the moment.

"It is that." Pride was in every line of Wilmore's body. "Been in our family about a hundred years or more. My granddaddy farmed most of the land around here until his death. My father sold off much of the land. He was a lawyer like me, you see. Reed and Reed on State Street, that's us. When my father died, he left the office and three houses to me and to Albert, Delphi's father. He also left the summer place and some vineyards up the road."

"Vineyards?" Micah asked as he followed Wilmore and listened to his description of Delphi's holdings. She followed after him, irate and mute.

"Yup. Grow some of the finest Delaware, Seyval, and Aurora in the state. Sell them to the Midstate Winery, mostly." Uncle Wilmore shrugged. "But times are hard for the New York grape growers, as you may have heard, and even though Delphi and I own shares in Midstate—"

"You have an interest in a winery?" Micah stopped his tour of the grounds.

Delphi stared at her uncle. "I never knew that."

"I was always afraid you might say something to your Aunt Jane about it." Wilmore grimaced. "And she nags me about enough things."

"Oh, Uncle Will." She kissed his cheek. "I'm glad you told her to oil the gate herself."

"So am I." He grinned at Delphi. Then he looked at Micah. "Well, young fella, I know you're quite a businessman. Saw your picture in *Forbes* magazine. So, what do you think of our summer place?"

Micah looked around him again. "I'd like to see the inside if I may."

"Don't be condescending." Delphi struck out at him, irritated with herself, because for a moment she had forgotten that she was angry with him.

He whirled around to lance her with his eyes. "I was not being condescending. I was trying to assess your property."

"Don't think you can get your hands on this!" Delphi shouted at him unfairly, then could have bitten her tongue. "That was uncalled for." She looked away from him. "I apologize."

"You damn well should apologize." Micah leaned forward, his nostrils flaring, his eyebrows a quivering ebony bridge over his nose. "When have I ever given you the idea that I would take anything from you?"

"Never, but—"

"But, nothing," he grated out before looking over at an interested Wilmore, whose head slewed back

and forth between Delphi and Micah. "I would like
to see the inside of the house, please."

They entered the back hall which housed the
pantry and cold storage used before refrigeration.
Dishes and pans were hung on walls and ceilings
and there were cupboards and shelves on both
sides of the narrow room. Past that was the great
room that combined a roomy kitchen area with
slatted wooden cupboards and tile-topped coun-
ters. Through the opening of the hanging cupboards and the worktop could be seen the large
dining area that had floor-to-ceiling windows, as
did the living room. The view out onto the lake was
panoramic both north and south and, when the
windows were opened, the whole front area of the
house would be like a porch.

"The original Reed homestead burned down in
my father's time and when it was rebuilt, it was
just used as a summer place because by that time,
Grandfather Reed was dead and father was not
farming," Wilmore said, looking around him with
a fond expression on his face. "There's a mite more
cleaning to do before you move in, Delphi, but the
place isn't in too bad shape. Shall we go upstairs?"
Wilmore moved toward a wide staircase.

"You are planning to live here?" Micah spoke
through clenched teeth, his fingers closing on
Delphi's upper arm.

She pulled and tugged at his fingers. "This is my
home. Of course I'm going to live here."

"Your home is with me."

"You two coming?" Uncle Wilmore called down
the stairs.

"Yes, Uncle, *I'm* coming," Delphi called,
wrenching her arm free and running up the stairs
to the square hall that had three doors leading off
it.

"Child, I thought you would prefer the front

room. It's the biggest one and it has the view of the lake." Wilmore led her into the spacious room that had radiators disguised with painted metal tops.

She nodded. "I remember this room." She inhaled the familiar smell of camphor, peppermint, and polishing oil. "Uncle, you have worked so hard. Who helped you?"

"The Adamses, James and Philomena, worked down here every day. Do you remember them?"

Delphi frowned for a moment. "Wait. She was a schoolteacher . . ."

Wilmore nodded. "So was James. Both been retired for years. She was the one who brought down the canned peaches and raspberries for your shelf and stocked the freezer for you."

"That's good," Micah's baritone rolled through the air. "Then we won't have to shop right away."

"We?" Delphi bristled, then gulped when he whirled to face her, teeth bared.

"Yes. We." He thundered the words.

Delphi thought she saw the sheer flowered curtains move at the force of his voice.

"Think you'll like it here?" Wilmore inquired.

"I'll get used to it," Micah replied.

"You'll hate it!" Delphi panted, squeezing her hands together in front of her. "And don't think I'll stand for your complaints. You can't stay here."

"Drop it, Delphi."

Wilmore blinked at her. "He says drop it, dear child."

"I heard him," she said testily to her uncle, then she lowered her voice. "But he will hate it here and want to leave in two days, maybe less."

"Stop mumbling. Your uncle is showing me the rest of the bedrooms. Then we'll finish the cleaning. Then we'll go back to the Gould Hotel and get our things. . . ." He was still instructing when Delphi glared at him, arms akimbo.

"This is not Steele Associates. You are not the boss here," she barked, feeling her chin jut forward.

Micah stared at her. The silence lengthened. Wilmore rubbed his jaw with one hand, gazing out the window toward the lake.

"You are not running things here," she said in a less strident tone.

"No, my sweet, I am not, but neither are you getting me to leave this place. I am making arrangements this morning to move my office from New York to here." He turned his powerful body toward Wilmore. "I suppose there are people in the town who can be hired for office work?"

Uncle Wilmore led the way out of the master bedroom into the hall again. "Well, times are hard." He shook his head. "The Milburn girl went to a business school in Rochester but she hasn't had much luck. She's a cocktail waitress at the moment." Wilmore rolled his eyes toward Delphi as she followed the two men into the huge bathroom with separate shower stall that she didn't remember and the monstrous cast-iron tub on claw feet that she did. The commode was on a pedestal so that it was necessary to go up one step to use it. There was even a pull chain above the toilet. The floor was tiled in sea green and the wallpaper was apple green with pink roses. It was quaint and Delphi remembered it with love.

"I'm glad you've never changed the wallpaper, Uncle Wilmore," she whispered.

"Wouldn't do that. Your grandmother brought that back from France. Real linen it is. She insisted that her bathroom be a proper one for a lady." He gazed at the shower stall. "Of course, I don't know what she would have said about that. Ladies were supposed to hide themselves under bubbles, not stand up when they were bathing."

Delphi laughed and Micah swung to look at her. "Your face is thinner. Have you been dieting?" His soft snarl was like a lariat, encircling her, holding her in place so that he could stare at her.

"No. I haven't been dieting." Delphi put a hand up to her face, aware that, as her body had filled out, her face had thinned somewhat. She held her breath that he wouldn't notice how tight her jeans were, even though they were a size larger than the ones she normally wore. She blessed the flannel shirt she tied around her middle, the ties falling down in front of her waist and, she hoped, acting as a camouflage to her middle.

They gave the two smaller bedrooms cursory inspection, then headed down the stairs and out into the front yard.

Almost at once, a large golden dog bounded across the beach toward them.

Micah took hold of Delphi's arm and put her behind him as the galloping behemoth charged.

"Not to worry . . . just a puppy." Wilmore whistled and slapped his leg and the dog gamboled up to him, rising to put his hamlike paws on Wilmore's chest. The strength of the dog rocked the slight man. "Easy, boy. Down, now, Question. Good dog."

"Question?" Delphi peeked around Micah, then when she saw the lolling tongue, the velvet brown eyes rolling her way, she stepped around him to pat the exuberant dog. When the dog would have jumped on Delphi, Micah caught his front paws and pushed him down again.

"Sit," he commanded. The dog sat . . . for twenty seconds. Then he bounded up again and tried to lick Delphi's hand.

"Uncle Wilmore, he's a darling. Is he yours?"

"Guess so. I found him here on the beach near the end of winter, half starved and near frozen. I wanted to take him home, but Jane wouldn't have the dog in the house. So, I kept him out here. I was coming out here every day to work anyway, just to get away from the house, and I kept the dog in the little shed off the kitchen. I put in a pet door for him when he got used to the place and made a run for him. See?" Wilmore pointed to the enclosure on the north side of the house that was fenced on the road side, but open to the water and the small pet door in the shed.

"Won't he swim around and get away?" Micah patted the dog but would not let him jump on Delphi or himself.

"For some reason the critter is afraid of water. That's strange, too, because he does have retriever in him. His feet are webbed and he has that extra coat, but I can't coax him near the water." Wilmore pointed to the south side of the property where he had another fence down to the water's edge. "I was going to open up the area so that he had the entire beach to run in. Poor boy, he needs a good home."

"Since I'm going to live here, I'll keep him with me," Delphi told her uncle, crouching down in front of the dog crooning to it. "He'll be company for me."

"For us," Micah said in a harsh whisper. "I'll be here when your friend shows up, Delphi."

"I have no friend coming."

"She doesn't. She would have said something," Wilmore pointed out mildly.

Micah stared at the man, then his eyes narrowed on Delphi. "There is no other man," he stated in low tones.

"I said that." Delphi lifted her chin as he stared at her. When she saw his smile break, his eyes melt into the velvet she had been used to seeing when he looked at her, she gulped a deep breath.

"Damn you, woman. I will find out why you left

me." The words whistled from his throat right into her flesh.

Delphi broke from the hypnotic pull of his eyes and looked at her uncle, her thoughts tumbling through her mind. "Ah . . . Uncle, why did you call the dog Question?"

"Well . . ." Wilmore led the way back through the house after they made their good-byes to the mournful dog. "I know he has golden retriever in him because of his color and web feet, but he's so big and broad in the shoulder and his hindquarters are so wide, that I think he might have Great Pyrenees in him too. But it's a question." His eyes twinkled at his niece, who laughed back. They had reached the cars and he turned to Micah, who was watching Delphi. "Listen, dear, as long as you have Micah here to help you with your things, why don't I stay here and start waxing that kitchen floor as I had planned to do today?"

"No . . . I—" Delphi began.

"That would be a good idea, Will," Micah stated, opening Delphi's car door. He stared at the car and scowled. "I'll have your own car sent from New York. We can return this today. I don't like you driving rented cars."

"Yours is rented," Delphi pointed out as he closed her door and leaned in the window.

He kissed her nose. "That's different. Executive cars are kept in first-class shape."

"So are—"

"Don't argue." He walked around and got in his car, flapped his hand at Wilmore, then started the car, spun the wheels, and headed back down the drive to the Oak Beach Road.

"Damn him." Delphi frowned at her grinning uncle as she started the Skylark and turned carefully in the widened end of the drive in front of the barn. "All he ever does is interrupt me," she grum-

bled as she drove down the beach road to the highway. "God, how can I leave him again? But how
can I stay with him? Oh damn, damn, damn! I
wish I didn't love him. I'd tell him to take a hike."
She muttered all the way back to the Seneca Falls
and the hotel.

She saw Micah bent over the trunk of the
Mercedes, placing items of clothing in it. She
ignored him as she turned into a space across from
his in the parking lot, but when she went to open
her door, he was there to do it, then help her out of
the vehicle.

"I've already talked to the hotel people. They will
take care of returning your car, darling." He leaned
down to kiss her mouth, his tongue tasting her
inner lip.

She felt her whole body shudder, then she was
pushing him away. "Why . . . why the sudden
change?" she gasped, her eyes slanting sideways
as she saw a man pause on State Street to look at
them. "Micah, this is a small town, not Manhattan. People are staring."

"Let them. As for the change, it's because I've
decided you really didn't leave me for another
man."

"That's true." Delphi gulped as his hand closed
on her breast. "Micah!"

"That bothered me a lot . . . and I intend to find
out why you left me. If it wasn't for another man,
then for what? Care to tell me now?"

She opened her mouth, then shook her head,
looking up at him and not knowing how to tell him
. . . or if she should tell him, but even if she didn't
and he wouldn't leave her—

"Damn you, my darling Delphi. I will find out
why you left me. How dare you chew me up and spit
me out like that?" His mind churned, even though
he schooled his features. He was furious with her,

but he had lived with her too long not to realize that he found out more by playing a waiting game than any other method. "I liked the note you sent me."

"Did you?"

"Yes, my darling, I liked it very much and I'm going to keep it . . . for many reasons." He kissed the top of her head. "Now let's go up and get our things together."

"Hello, Delphinium. How are you, dear? It's Mrs. Cramer." The elderly lady waved her hand.

Delphi tried to shake loose of Micah's hold, but he wouldn't release her.

He led her toward the senior citizen, his hand clamped at her waist. "How do you do, Mrs. Cramer? I'm Micah Steele."

"Oh, are you Delphinium's young man?"

"Yes, I am. Delphi and I were wondering if you would join us for dinner next week here in the hotel? Say next Wednesday?"

Mrs. Cramer beamed. "That would be lovely. Wednesday would be fine."

"We'll see you then. We'll call and let you know what time we'll pick you up." Micah gave her his most charming smile.

The older lady lifted her chin, humming to herself as she walked down State Street to her home.

"That was nice of you, Micah. She is really very sweet and has known Uncle Wilmore for years." Delphi hadn't even realized she had been leaning on him until she turned toward the hotel again.

"Don't pull away, love, you need me . . . and I need you."

"Micah, please."

"Not to worry. We'll do it your way . . . for a while, until you begin to trust me again."

Her head whipped up until she was staring into

his eyes. "It wasn't that I didn't trust you . . ." Her voice faltered.

Anger slashed like lightning across his face and then was gone. His jaw moved like a concrete block, then was still. "You don't trust me . . . now, Delphi. I'll find out why, then we'll go on from there." He left her and strode out of the parking lot.

Delphi hurried after him, along the street and up the steps into the small lobby. She smiled weakly at the manager as he came forward to speak to her, seeing Micah disappear into the elevator, the metal cage door closing behind him.

"Miss Reed . . . your husband, Mr. Steele, said that you would be checking out this morning." He beamed. "But he said that you were both pleased with the Gould Hotel and would be coming back to stay some other time." He coughed. "Ah . . . do you use your maiden name because you're an author? Or an actress?"

"No." Delphi was nonplussed. "I'm a model and—"

"Ah . . ." He looked sagacious. "Now I understand." He cocked his head, smiled and turned and went into the dining room.

"Do you?" Delphi mumbled. "I wish I did." She went over to the elevator and pressed the button. In seconds she was rising to the third floor.

The door to her room was open. Micah was in there packing her clothes. "Micah, I can do that."

"I know, but I wanted to help." He turned around and looked at her, his smile running over her like hot lava. "I like this town and I like the Gould Hotel."

"Susan B. Anthony made her first speech for women's rights around the corner," Delphi stated, feeling a shyness with him all at once.

"Did she now? Wise of her to pick such a nice area."

"Yes." They stared at each other for long moments. The dust motes dancing in a sunbeam formed the single barrier between them. "I . . . I'll get the toiletries from the bathroom."

"All right, darling."

The word "darling" stopped her dead in the doorway to the short hall that led to the bathroom and lounge. She felt as though her shoes were nailed to the floor. Without turning, she swallowed and spoke. "Things change, Micah. They can't always be the way we want them to be."

"Delphi, get your things." The velvet of his voice was a cocoon for her.

She ran for the bathroom.

In short order, she was packed.

Micah looked at the small amount of luggage she was carrying. "This isn't one-eighth of your clothes." He looked over at her. "I've sent for the rest and informed Charine that you would need new recreation wear and to send it on."

"Micah, listen, there is something I must tell you."

"There are many things you have to tell me, and tonight after I've lit a nice fire in that fireplace at The Embers you can begin, but not now. It's time to go."

They checked out with a minimum of fuss because as usual Micah received the royal treatment that he had come to expect wherever he went.

To his credit, Delphi mused, he always treated people with respect. And it got him the earth, she reflected as everyone in the lobby seemed to want to say good-bye to Micah. How did he always do it?

"Ready, darling?" Micah turned and so did a host of heads.

"Yes."

"I've told Mr. Flynn of our dinner plans for next

Wednesday for the five of us and he says that eight-thirty is fine for dinner."

Delphi was silent until Micah ushered her into the Mercedes, then went around to climb under the wheel. She craned her neck, looking for the Buick Skylark that she had rented. It was gone. "Micah, who are the five of us?"

"Mrs. Cramer, your aunt and uncle and us."

"Micah, my aunt might not come. She doesn't like me . . . sometimes I don't think she likes my uncle either."

"We'll see." He lifted one shoulder, checked the mirror, and drove out of the parking lot. "I think I'm going to like it here in Seneca Falls."

"You'll be bored in three days, you Big Apple-ite, you Manhattan groundhog," Delphi sputtered.

"Not true, darling." Micah put his hand on her knee and squeezed in slow rhythm. "I could never be bored in any place when you were with me."

"Micah," Delphi's tone was wheedling, "you should go back to New York."

"Forget it unless you're prepared to come with me. I'm not going anywhere without you. Whatever the hell it is you're hiding from me is not going to make one bit of difference, either. So stop carping about my leaving here." The steering wheel of the Mercedes seemed to leap beneath his hand as he roared across the bridge over the Seneca River and swung east toward the lake.

"Micah, stop at that market, please. They have lovely Italian bread and rolls and we can get some staples." Delphi's fingernails dug into his arm as the car made a sweeping right turn and bounced into the parking lot.

A battered Chevy and a Ford station wagon screeched to a halt as Micah blithely whizzed by them into an open space not far from the door.

Delphi closed her eyes. "You will be the cause of

my being tarred and feathered in this county, I know it."

"What are you mumbling about, sweetheart?" Micah turned in his seat, his right arm along the back, his fingers touching Delphi's cheek.

She looked at him, absolutely sure he didn't even notice the irate persons walking past the car, glowering at him. He hadn't looked away from her. "Nothing. Would you like to wait in the car while—"

"No. I'm coming with you." He opened his door, stepped out and stretched, the handwoven cotton shirt he wore pulling taut over his muscular chest.

When she saw a woman carrying one bag of groceries to her car pause, then thrust out her chest and backside to stroll slowly past Micah, Delphi had a strong desire to get out and drop-kick the woman in the part of her jeans that said LEE.

Micah opened her door and reached in to help her from the car. She came out against his chest, her hands reaching up to hold him, her mouth grazing his chin.

Micah followed Delphi's sideways glance and noticed the woman in jeans. Why, the little witch was staking her claim! She was jealous! Good, he thought, it was nice not to be the only one with that affliction. "Hellcat," he whispered in her ear.

"She ought to be ashamed of herself carrying on that way." Delphi moved away from him, not pretending to misunderstand his shout of laughter as he followed her into the store.

It gave Delphi a sense of quiet delight to watch Micah take things from the shelf and put them in the basket—even if they were wildly inappropriate.

"Don't frown at me. A jar of caviar will come in handy when we entertain."

He had said *when*, not if. Delphi silently damned him and herself. She'd never be able to leave him again. She'd just have to wait until he booted her out like the other ones. She felt like a martyr. She refused to listen to the little voice in her brain that told her that when Micah had "booted" out his other wives and mistresses, he had settled enough money on them to make them independent for life. She knew that no amount of money could ever compensate for Micah's love. And she was sure she wouldn't be able to take anything from him. She inhaled a miserable breath. At least their contract was good for something. She could refuse any money Micah tried to give her.

Six

Life took on a pattern at The Embers. Micah would work most mornings, in contact with London, New York, Tokyo by phone. Delphi found many chores to do around the place. She made new curtains for all the upstairs bedrooms and bought new quilts. Not all Micah's protestations changed her mind about making the curtains. He surprised her by telling her that he was having a wing built on the first floor that would be theirs. The master bedroom upstairs would become a guest room just like the others when the new wing was completed.

He informed her of all this one evening by the fire, the night after the dinner party with her aunt and uncle and Mrs. Cramer at the Gould. "It will give us more privacy, darling, and I can have the hot tub installed. You like it so much. A sauna too. We'll have our own sitting room and big bedroom and it will all look out on the lake."

She was cuddled in the curve of his arm,

watching the fire. She looked up at him, feeling a sting of tears in her eyes. "Micah, that's a wonderful idea. Darling, we've had so many interruptions all this week and last—moving, staining the outside of the cottage—and we haven't had our little talk."

"It sounds like a big talk to me," Micah murmured into her hair.

"It is." She freed herself from his hold and sat straighter on the couch, looking down at her clenched hands, then back up to his face. "Micah, I'm expecting a child." She looked down again and swallowed hard when she heard the hiss of his breath and his muttered, "So that's it." "I have no intention of having an abortion. I want the child and intend to raise it by myself."

Micah jumped from the couch and paced back and forth, his chest heaving as though he had run the Boston Marathon. "No bloody way are you raising this child alone." He pronounced each word slowly, every syllable underlined by his sibilant breath. "We are getting married—now!" Blood gushed through his veins and arteries, pounding violently through his heart. Delphi was going to have his child! He would make her marry him! Elation, like adrenaline, sent his heartbeat into overdrive. "I'll make the arrangements right away, love."

"No." Delphi leaped to her feet. She could feel emotion warring within her. "I . . . I'm glad you want to stay with me, but no marriage. You'd hate it. You'd want out . . . and . . . and I don't believe in divorce. I won't live with that hanging over my head."

Micah's mouth fell open as he saw the tormented expression on her face. "Darling, listen to me. I know we signed that agreement about no marriage, but just listen, please. I want this child too. And I want us to be a family."

"Micah . . ." Delphi felt the tears streaming from her eyes. "I can't. You'd hate it . . . and . . . and even if you tried to hide it from me, I'd know. . . ."

"Delphi, sweetheart." Micah felt a helpless anger. "I love you, Del. You know that."

She nodded her head, tears still splashing down her cheeks. "I never cry, you know." She gulped, swiping the back of her hand at her cheek.

"I know," he said softly, never feeling so impotent in his life. "Honey, please don't make these sweeping statements about us yet. We'll talk to a . . . a minister . . ." He couldn't remember if they had ever talked about religion but he assumed that she had belonged to a church at one time.

"I'm a Catholic," she said. "We talked about everything under the sun but religion. . . ." She gave a huge shuddering sigh.

"I was baptized into the Greek religion of my mother, but I have not attended church in years," he said softly.

"After I lost . . ." She pressed her hand to her abdomen, and looked up at him, wide-eyed.

He reached her in one long stride. "Nothing is going to happen to you or the baby," he vowed, embracing her, his hand rubbing along her spine from neck to coccyx. "I'll take care of you, married or unmarried . . . always. . . ."

Delphi lifted her finger to his mouth. "Mustn't say always. We don't make commitments."

"The game rules have just changed, my darling." He leaned back from her. "The campaign has begun to prove to you that what I want with you is a lifetime together. Our child, you, me . . . together."

"And Dory and Paul." Delphi sighed again, cuddling to his chest. "I like being their 'Moms.' "

She clapped her hand over her mouth and looked up at him, seeing the triumph in his face, in the upthrust of his chin. "That doesn't mean that I'll marry you."

"I won't pressure you into anything, but I am going to arrange to talk to the priest at St. Patrick's Church. . . ."

Delphi's head snapped up. "How did you know that was the name of the church in Seneca Falls?"

Micah grinned at her. "While I was waiting to be checked into the Gould Hotel, I read a newspaper that mentioned the church."

And his mind was like a giant repository, Delphi thought. It never lost anything it took in. She shook her head and rubbed her face on his neck. "There is a church closer than that. Holy Cross Church is in Ovid, about eight miles from here."

"Good. I'll check out both of them." He leaned down and lifted her and walked back to the couch and sat down, cradling her close. "Darling, are you well? Are you under the care of a competent doctor?"

"Yes, to both questions. Of course I have to drive into Rochester for my monthly checkups."

"What?" Micah hugged her tighter. "No way. I'll have a plane sent down here. I'll pilot you in when you need to go to the doctor."

"Micah, that's so extravagant."

"Delphi, I'll send a huge check to World Hunger, or to Greenpeace, or to anything else you want me to, but I *will* be flying you to Rochester."

Delphi opened her mouth and shut it again when she saw the bulldog look on Micah's face.

"Sweetheart," Micah said after a few silent moments, "what does the doctor say about our making love? Will it be all right?"

"You've been a papa twice before and you don't

know? Shame on you." Delphi laughed when she saw the run of blood up his face.

"It never mattered before. Nothing ever mattered too much until you came into my life. Didn't you know that?" His eyes bored into hers as she lay across his lap. "Oh, I loved Dory and Paul and was proud of them, but I never felt the exhilarating love for them that I have now . . . and that's because you taught me about sunrises, my darling. Remember? *When your face appeared over my crumpled life at first I understood only the poverty of what I have.* That's me, Delphi. I met you and it was a blinding light that almost burned me to a cinder. I was so damned far gone, lady mine, that I wasn't sure that even you could get me out of that arid pit that was my life. *I am so frightened of the unexpected sunrise finishing.* Stay with me, Del. Don't take it away."

"Micah . . . Micah . . ." Her voice rose higher as she clutched him to her.

He carried her to bed that night and they undressed each other with slow silent care, looking at each other's body with mutual enjoyment. "You are still my darling." Micah's voice seemed to come from deep inside him.

"And you are my Micah," Delphi said dreamily as he slipped her briefs from her body. She lifted weighted eyelids to watch him touch her tummy with gentle strokes. "What are you doing, Micah?"

"Saying hello to our baby." He kissed her navel, his teeth nipping at the tender folds there. "What a beautiful baby!"

"Don't be silly." Delphi lifted a heavy arm and pushed at the strand of black hair falling forward on his face. "How could you know how the baby will look?"

"Could we produce anything that wasn't beautiful? No. Even if our child was not perfect to others, he would be to us. I will love him. I love him now. . . ." His husky voice was buried in her abdomen. Even as he slid lower he muttered love words to both Delphi and the baby.

"He?" she asked him, her mind ballooning with the love she felt for him. "What if it's a girl?"

"I love little girls, especially if they have red hair and silver-green eyes." He looked up at her, the sensual sleepiness of his eyes exciting her as always.

Delphi felt his tongue touch lower on her, then gently enter her. Her body arched and a keening sound issued from her throat. "Micah . . . Micah . . ."

"Right with you all the way, precious. . . ." His guttural voice reached her as he came back up her body and entered her with even more than his usual gentleness, taking her, yet holding back, loving her, yet cherishing her. The soothing furnace erupted around them and even then Micah was careful.

She gripped him as both passion and impatience filled her. "I want you," she told him in clear, loud words.

Micah couldn't withstand her power and he came to her groaning and filling her with love.

The world spilled away and they were alone on a jet stream climb to oneness, the light too bright to let the world in, the heat burning away thoughts of that outer world.

They lay face to face, mouth to mouth, their breathing slowly coming back to normal, their eyes opening almost at the same time.

"You are so beautiful, Micah."

"You are my sweet pudding."

They laughed and hugged each other, delighted that they could play their little love games again.

Delphi sighed and snuggled closer, then her eyes

popped open. "You're forty-two," she said softly into the silence filling the room.

Micah turned to look at her, a wariness in the lazy look he gave her. "True. And I will be forty-three in September. Why the surprise?"

"You can't want to marry again and start a family," she said, an agonized expression on her face. Kissing the hair that surrounded the nipple on his chest, she murmured, "You will be so bored, feel so trapped."

Micah lifted her over his body so that her hair fell around them both. "Why are you being so stubborn about this? I want to marry you. I want our child . . . and if you say I'm too old to be a father, I'll paddle your bottom as I should have done when you first ran from me. Now get it through your head—we are getting married, and if you decide to divorce me, you can do it on our sixtieth wedding anniversary!"

"Silly." Delphi laid her cheek on his chest, relief flowing through her. She lifted her head again. "You didn't tell me how you found me so fast."

For a moment, Micah's hands clenched on her. "I called you when Larry and I arrived at the site. Then I called you again from the hotel, several times. When the housekeeper said she hadn't seen you all day, I called Wolf and Kenny." He gnashed his teeth. "After talking to them, I flew home at once. On the way, I called Renson. He's a detective the firm has used on occasion. By the time I arrived home, Renson had a few answers for me. Your credit card and phone calls left a pretty good trail, darling. Then I remembered that you had relatives in Seneca Falls by the name of Reed."

She raised her head again. "However did you remember that? I couldn't have mentioned Uncle Wilmore's hometown more than once."

"I recall most things you've said to me, sweetheart. I have a special file on you deep inside of me." Micah's smile was crooked, but his onyx eyes told her he was serious.

"I didn't want to hurt you." Her hand came up to stroke his forehead as she looked down at him. "I love you and didn't want you to be forced into anything."

"And have I seemed unhappy to you? Even one moment of our time together?"

"No." The word was a whisper of sound.

"I will be very unhappy if you don't marry me and stay with me. Do you want to make me happy?"

"Yes."

"Then don't leave me. Don't let 'the colors in my eyes vanish' that Yevtushenko spoke of. . . ." His voice had turned rough as sandpaper with emotion.

"Oh, love, love!" Delphi clutched him, tears splashing down on him.

"You're drowning me, precious." He nuzzled her.

"I'm so silly with this pregnancy." She pushed back from him. "But I don't have morning sickness. That was one of the things that fooled me. With the other pregnancy, I was so sick all the time. . . ."

Micah felt her hands clutch at him. She was afraid! The knowledge filled him with leonine possessiveness, leonine protectiveness. "This baby will be fine, my sweet. I will be taking care of you."

"I know."

"Darling, you are having an instant effect on me again," Micah growled at her, making her laugh. "Circe, you did that on purpose."

"I cannot tell a lie," Delphi said unctuously, a giggle rising in her throat.

"Pay the piper," Micah told her, pressing her body to his aroused one, then gently turning her onto her back. "I am going to love taking care of you."

"I think I might like it too." Delphi undulated her hips against his body.

"Delphi, stop! Wait! Let me love you first." Micah groaned heavily.

She felt an enormous surge of feminine power as his control began to slip. She wanted to give and give to Micah. He had always given her so much. Far from letting him go, she continued to caress him and kiss his face and neck.

Both were moaning when he entered her, the love cycle taking them again.

They fell asleep as they almost always did with their arms wrapped around one another.

When Delphi opened her eyes, sun was streaming across the silvery rippled water. She sat up in bed, frowned at the indentation of the pillow where Micah's head had been, then stretched and yawned.

The bedroom door opened and Micah was standing there with a tray. "Good morning, darling. I've brought your breakfast."

"You're spoiling me." It was a delight to see him in a sports shirt and cut-off jeans with beach clogs on his feet instead of the Savile Row suits and Italian leather shoes he usually wore on a weekday.

"Your hair is wet. Have you showered?" Delphi sniffed at the tea he'd brought her instead of coffee, the large glass of orange juice, the two slices of cholla bread with sweet butter on it and—she lifted the metal cover on another bowl—"Oatmeal?"

"Yes. I talked to the doctor over the phone and then I called Sara and they told me that whole-grain cereals were good for you. See. I've brought a peach to slice over the cereal."

"I haven't eaten oatmeal since I was five years old," she said in fading accents as she watched him pour milk into the bowl.

"No brown sugar or homogenized milk, and I used very little salt. Pregnant women don't need salt," he said pedantically.

"Oh." Delphi watched the spoon come toward her mouth, wondering if she would hate it. She opened up and closed her eyes, the warm oats heating her all the way to her stomach. "It's not bad," she informed Micah, startled. "But I can feed myself."

"I know . . . but I like feeding you."

She chuckled, then pressed two fingers to her lips when she saw his serious mien. "Don't you have calls to make? Other than to doctors?"

Micah looked at his watch. "I have fifteen minutes before my first call. What are you going to do today?"

Delphi swallowed another spoonful of oatmeal, amazed that she liked such unattractive food. "I'm going into Seneca Falls to visit Mrs. Cramer and have lunch. She has been wanting me to come. Darling, are you going to call Dory and Paul about coming to the lake?"

"Yes. Darling, don't think badly of me, but much as I want to see them, I'm going to miss our absolute privacy."

"Poor baby." Delphi patted his head. "Darling, you should have dried your hair after your shower. It's still wet."

"I haven't showered yet. I went swimming." Micah grinned at her.

Delphi sat straighter, placing the tray on the bedside table. "Are you telling me that you went swimming in Cayuga Lake in June? Alone? With no one around?" Her voice was rising to a shriek as she pictured him going down in the frigid water and not surfacing again. "Micah . . ." she wailed, clutching at him.

"Now, sweetheart, don't. I wouldn't have told you

if I'd thought you'd feel this way. I only went out waist-high and swam a short way. It isn't that cold. It's June and the water is heating up."

"Promise me if you want to go swimming, you'll wake me up so that I can watch you. Promise."

"Question was with me. I mean Bear. I'm glad we renamed him Bear. I didn't like—"

"Micah, promise me!" Delphi's voice was shrill.

"I promise, sweetheart, I promise." He felt a stab of guilt as he looked at her tear-wet eyes. Tears were never far from the surface these days, he knew that, but he still never meant to upset her this way. She did love him, he thought, and his heart began to thunder in his chest. God, he didn't want to live in a world without her. He stretched himself out on the bed next to her, taking her into his arms. "No more scares, angel, I promise."

Delphi sniffled and a shudder passed through her body. "Good. Micah, I can't lose you now." Her eyes still dewy, she looked up at him. "I haven't the strength to lose you twice." She lifted her finger to touch his chin. "Will you please outlive me, Micah?" she asked softly.

"Darling . . . Delphi . . ." His mind reeled as he hugged her to him. "Angel, don't talk like that."

"Please. You know I never ask you for things."

He shook his head. "No, you never ask me for anything." Irritation flashed across his face and was gone. "But, darling, surely you can see—"

"You can take care of yourself . . . not drink too much, take your vitamins, exercise . . ." Delphi looked thoughtful. "Of course swimming and lifting weights at your club is very good."

"I'll do everything I can to make sure I live to be one hundred. . . ."

"At least. In this day and age, that's not so much."

"All right," Micah said and smiled. "I'll try for one hundred and ten."

"Thank you."

"You're welcome." He kissed her, then pulled back and scowled at his watch. "I have to make those calls, darling. Listen, I would rather you drove the Mercedes instead of your Sport. You'd be safer."

"But, Micah, you might need it."

He shrugged, rising from the bed, kissing her again, then heading for the door. "I have the truck . . . or in a pinch I can squeeze into your car. The workmen are coming today to do some interior work on our new wing. I want to be free when they're doing it."

"God help them." Delphi laughed at him and blew him a kiss.

"Have more respect, woman," he growled at her, his eyes alight with laughter.

When he left, she hopped out of bed, grimacing in the mirror when she saw her distended middle. "You are getting so big, so fast, Delphi Reed. It's a good thing you canceled all your contracts."

She dressed in a long-waisted cotton dress in navy blue with a nautical collar. It masked her tummy and was very comfortable to wear. She donned the light hip-length cotton jacket in navy and white cotton that matched the dress, gazed critically in the mirror at her flat-heeled navy shoes and blue stockings. She wondered if that above-the-knee style was outré in Seneca Falls. She lifted a shoulder, still looking at her image. It would be with Aunt Jane, for sure. She'd just pray she didn't run into her if Mrs. Cramer wanted to walk down Fall Street.

She drove into town in the Mercedes, loving the muted roar of power under the hood and all the lovely accessories within the car. Delphi listened to the stereo and hummed along with Barbra Streisand.

Once in town, she slowed to the speed limit and drove to State Street and the lovely old home that belonged to Mrs. Cramer.

Delphi knew at once by the coin-sized spots of red on Mrs. Cramer's cheeks and the extra sparkle in her eyes as she answered the door, that the elderly lady had news she was bursting to share.

"Delphi, my dear, you will never guess. A Women's Coalition has come to town and I have invited two of the women to have tea with us."

Mystified, Delphi followed her friend through the high-ceilinged home to an enclosed room Mrs. Cramer referred to as the solarium. Two women dressed in smart linen suits looked her way and smiled.

"Mrs. Devere, this is Delphi Reed, soon to be Delphi Steele—" Mrs. Cramer clapped her hand to her mouth. "Unless you are going to keep your own name as some girls do today."

"No. I'm going to take Micah's name," Delphi murmured, moving closer to shake Mrs. Devere's hand. "Hello."

"Hello. May I call you Delphi? It's such a pretty name. My name is Sally Devere and this is Helga Brinker from Holland who is in the European Women's Coalition for Peace."

"How do you do," Helga said in heavily accented English, her china-blue eyes glowing with warmth.

Delphi felt that Helga must be close to her own age, but Sally Devere had to be in her middle fifties. "I'm afraid I'll have to show my ignorance and admit I know nothing about your movement."

"We are here to demonstrate against the proliferation of nuclear arms, arms that we feel are stored at the Seneca Depot in Romulus, New York," Sally said firmly.

Helga nodded. Mrs. Cramer pressed her hands together and nodded once.

"The government neither confirms nor denies our allegations, which, of course, is par for the course," Sally said.

Helga nodded.

"I believe that they would have denied it unless the nuclear arms were there," Mrs. Cramer cheeped, drawing the heads of the other three her way.

"I see." Delphi felt her way, not too interested really, but curious to find out what would make a woman leave her home and take up such a cause.

"There is no future for us or our children if the world is jeopardized by these ever-increasing numbers of more and more sophisticated—and deadly—weapons," Sally said passionately.

Delphi blinked, then her hand crept to her abdomen. No future for her baby! "But what do you hope to accomplish?"

"We want to focus American thought on the dangers of stockpiling nuclear weapons. . . ."

The women talked all through lunch and for most of the afternoon.

Delphi drove home to Oak Beach Road fired with the resolve to do what she could to let the world know that the nuclear arms race promised man a bleak, threatened future. But she had an uncomfortable feeling that there was something she had forgotten.

As she prepared dinner that evening for Micah and herself, she could hardly contain herself. She wanted to tell him all about her afternoon and what the Women's Coalition would be doing at the Women's Peace Encampment.

He roared into the kitchen and caught her around the waist, lifting her off her feet into his arms. "What have I told you about overdoing?" he growled as he held her high, her body hanging down the length of his, her face just above his. He shook her gently, his teeth nipping at her chin. "I don't want you working like this. I am getting you a housekeeper."

Delphi felt her eyes well with tears, even though she wasn't feeling *that* sad. "Micah, I like making the meals."

"I know, sweetheart, but I don't want you rushing around, tiring yourself . . ." he soothed, his tongue lapping at the tears. "When Paul and Dory come, there will be that much more work around here. . . ."

"They are very helpful," Delphi defended her cubs.

"Yes, with you they are, but they are also forgetful and you have a habit of picking up after them." He kissed her nose. "I won't do anything to upset you, but your uncle says there is a widow, Mrs. Lentz, on the lake road who is a housekeeper. She and her two children are having a rough time since Eisenhower College closed and her employers had to let her go." He kissed her again. "It would be a kindness on your part, angel."

"You're blackmailing me, aren't you?"

"Yes, my treasure, I am. I know how you can't resist a poor soul, or a cause. I intend to see that you do not undertake too much during this pregnancy, and of course all causes are on hold until after the baby comes."

Delphi's tongue clove to the roof of her mouth. She wouldn't dare tell him about the Women's Coalition now. His eyes had that determined glitter. He would bellow like all the Bulls of Bashan if she tried to tell him that she wanted to take part in demonstrations in front of the Seneca Depot.

"Ah . . . would you like to toss the salad, love?" Delphi's eyes slid away from his penetrating stare.

"All right," Micah answered. "What is it, my sweet? Are you angry with me because I want to call this woman, Mrs. Lentz?"

"No." Delphi forced a smile. Damn him, he could read her so well. Hiding things from Micah was a major undertaking with small chance of success. "It would be nice to have her come in the mornings . . ."

"And I should pay her for all day. Right?" He chuckled.

"Yes, darling, you should." Delphi laughed with him, eager to redirect his attention. "I'll start the barbecue, Micah." She grinned at him. "I can't believe how fast you had that gas grill installed." She referred to the three-burner cooker and stove that Micah had ordered for them. Her uncle chortled about the way things got done at The Embers since Steele's arrival.

Dinner was broiled lobster tails, baked potatoes, and salad—simple fare with little fuss, but delicious.

She and Micah sat close together on the new front porch on their section of the house. It jutted out onto the beach and held a chaise longue in redwood with matching tables and two chairs, a dining alcove where they sat, and a couch swing that was as comfortable as a bed.

"You are a good cook, Mrs. Steele-to-be." Micah smiled at her, then fed her some spinach from his salad bowl.

"You have a wonderful appetite, Mr. Steele. You always have had, but it's even better now," Delphi said, pleased. "All that fresh air and—"

"Love," Micah finished, lifting her palm to his mouth. "You have given me everything, Delphinium Reed. Now I want you to give me one more thing."

"What?" Planets and stars went off in her head.

"Your hand in marriage, your vow of a lifetime with me as I will vow my lifetime with you. . . ." Micah spoke low.

"I want that too." She blinked the wetness back from her lashes.

He came around to her chair and lifted her from it, then tugged her gently over to the large swing to pull her down into his lap. "I talked to Father Conroy at St. Patrick's Church today and he said that our marriage could take place very soon and in the church since all of my marriages were civil ceremonies. We are to be married next Wednesday and unless you object I thought we would have Dory and Paul as our witnesses."

"Micah! That's wonderful!" Delphi sat up straighter. "What if they don't want . . . I mean, they might not want you to marry again." She shrugged, feeling her lips tremble.

"They already know because I told them that I wanted to marry you quite some time ago and that it would be for life." He kissed the nape of her neck then pulled her back into his arms again. "I am going to love being married to you, coming home to you every night of our lives, making love to you every night. . . ." Micah exhaled a deep sigh.

"I love you, darling," Delphi sniffed into his neck.

"For a girl who never cried, you are putting on some performance with this pregnancy." Micah grinned at her.

"Yes," Delphi wailed into his shoulder. "Isn't it awful?"

Micah was still chuckling as he lifted her into his arms and carried her upstairs.

"The dirty dishes," Delphi said feebly, her hand stroking his cheek.

"To hell with them."

Seven

Delphi was so excited about seeing Dory and Paul at the Seneca Falls airport, that when Micah's pilot landed in the twin-engine Cessna, she almost jumped up and down. "Micah, whose plane is that?"

"Mine, darling. I have two of them besides the Lear jet." He laughed out loud when she glared at him.

"Plutocrat," she snapped, then turned back to see Paul and Dory deplane. She hurried forward as they ran to her, the ready tears coursing down her cheeks.

They skidded to a stop in front of her, both mouths dropping open.

"Dad, what have you done to Moms?" Dory accused. "She never cries."

"She does now." Micah smirked at Delphi as he shook his son's hand. "Since she became pregnant, she weeps and wails at everything and nothing."

"Not true," Delphi sobbed.

"Ah, Moms. . . ." Paul looked at his father, alarmed. "Maybe it isn't good for her to be pregnant."

"It is too," Delphi gulped, hugging him and Dory at the same time. "I'm fine. It's just that—"

"She's like a lawn sprayer at the drop of a hat," Micah pointed out.

"Dad . . . really . . ." Dory glared at both her father and brother as they grinned at the sniffling Delphi.

"I'm so excited about the wedding," Dory exclaimed, resting her chin on the back of the front seat, Paul next to her. "I've never been in a wedding before." She sighed.

"Especially one between your father and your mother," Paul observed, exhibiting Micah's dry wit.

"I think it's wonderful," Dory said staunchly, irked when her father laughed with Paul. "What are you going to wear, Moms? Are you nervous? You should see the dress Charine made for me. It's a real zonk," she breathed.

"I'm not nervous," Delphi told her, then promptly felt her stomach flip-flop. "Well, not *too* nervous. Ah . . . my dress is a cream-colored silk, street length with an empire waistline." Delphi could feel the rush of blood to her face.

"Yes, I noticed that you were showing quite a bit," Paul stated.

"You're not supposed to say that, stupid. Besides, Moms wouldn't show so quickly if she wasn't so slender," Dory defended.

Paul nodded. "I didn't mean anything, Moms."

"I know that, darling." Delphi reached up and patted the hand on her shoulder.

"When is the wedding?" Dory asked.

"Tomorrow," Micah informed them.

"Tomorrow!" they chorused.

Delphi looked at Micah. "You didn't tell them when it was?"

"Sorry, darling. I didn't think." He smiled at her.

She wanted to berate him, but her mouth widened in an answering smile. She cast her mind into the future and pictured herself trying to tear into Micah. It wouldn't compute. Micah had her in thrall.

"Tonight we can stay home or go out for dinner at a very nice inn on the lake called Taughannock Farms Inn," Micah informed them as they headed off the highway to the lake road.

Delphi was sure that Paul and Dory weren't listening to their father as they pointed out the boats, both motor and sail. Delphi told Micah she'd prefer to stay at home for an intimate family dinner.

They drove down the private rutted road to the property and there was silence in the back seat until they pulled up and parked next to the barn.

"I've never been in a barn," Dory said in hushed tones.

"Is it all ours?" Paul asked.

"Yes." Delphi nodded. "Wait until you see." Before she could finish, Bear skidded around the barn and came at the car at a gallop.

"Damn fool," Micah muttered, jumping from the car and catching hold of the dog's front paws just as he would have jumped on the mirror finish of the Mercedes. "I am going to break you of that jumping habit," he muttered, then looked at Paul, whose mouth was open. Micah felt a wrenching guilt as he looked at his son and daughter. They'd never had a pet. Then he gazed at Delphi and saw the delight on her face at the way the two of them took to Bear.

"He's so big." Dory was cautious, then she began to laugh as the large dog put his paws on Paul's shoulders and started to lick his face. "He looks like a golden bear."

"That's his name," Delphi crowed. "Your father gave it to him. My uncle found him wandering on the beach and since my aunt won't allow dogs in her house, he kept him here."

Dory and Paul petted the dog and looked at Delphi at the same time. "Is he . . . will he have to go?" Dory voiced the question. Eighteen-year-old Paul had a tight, reserved mien.

"Not unless you want him to go. . . ." Delphi looked at Micah.

"We thought you might like to keep him . . . the two of you," Micah said, watching them, his throat closing when Paul whooped and Dory hugged the dog.

Bear jumped down and began racing around the car, then around the barn at breakneck speed.

"Look at him run . . ." Paul breathed, grinning. "He's really bookin'." Paul used one of the many "in" terms at his school.

"He sure is." Dory's head whipped around, her eyes glued to the dog.

Micah went over to Delphi and put his arm around her, bringing her close to his body. "The damn fool is liable to bowl you over . . ." he muttered.

"Look how happy they are with him!" Delphi gloated.

"You make them happy, Moms." Micah gazed at her, his heart pounding up in his throat at her beauty. "You are one delicious lady and I love you." He kissed her mouth. "And don't start crying again." He lapped at the one tear with his tongue.

He lifted his head. "Come on, you two, play with that goof later. Let's get these bags unpacked."

Dory and Paul kept the dog at their side all the while they carted their many things to the house.

"Is the water warm enough to swim, Dad?" Paul asked.

"It's getting there." Micah grinned at Delphi when she frowned at him. "Moms didn't like me going into the cold water, but with the heat we've been having, I think there will be swimming every day for all of us."

Dory hugged Delphi. "I love it here. When we used to go to camp, we never had such a big lake."

"And you could swim only at certain times," Paul added.

"Well, I'll want you to have a few rules here too." Delphi bit her lip.

Paul hugged her with one arm and with the other lugged a gym bag with tennis racket and other paraphernalia jutting from every opening. "Don't worry, Moms. We'll be careful and we'll abide by the rules."

Dory nodded, her eyes snapping with excitement as she was shown into her room.

Delphi stood in the upstairs hall with her arms around Micah's waist, his hand stroking her hair. "They like it, Micah . . . ohhh, look at him. How did he get in here?" Delphi pointed and laughed as Bear jumped up the stairs three at a time and barreled into Paul's room.

"That damn fool . . ." Micah growled, about to move into the room.

"Don't, darling. Let's go downstairs and let them handle Bear. I think they belong to him now." She chuckled.

Micah sighed and looked down at her, shaking his head at the serene look on her face. "You really don't mind that they have the dog up here, do you?"

"No . . . but I'm going to tell them that they have to clean their own rooms and make sure there is no hair around. I don't expect Mrs. Lentz to pick up after them or that elephant dog."

Micah nodded, freed himself from her hold; and walked into Paul's room. "Dory, will you come in here, please?"

Delphi could hear the low rise and fall of their voices, then Micah came out, his face wreathed in smiles.

"I should have asked for much more. They're so anxious to keep the dog with them, they would have agreed to paint the house."

Delphi snapped her fingers. "What a great idea." She laughed, then took his arm as he led her to the stairs, preceding her but still holding fast to her arm.

"The men are coming today to put the paneling in our sitting room in the new wing and the painters will be here tomorrow."

"Too bad." Delphi grinned at him. "You might have gotten Paul and Dory to do it."

Micah smiled and lifted her down the last step. "What are you going to do for the rest of the day? Fuss over the things you'll be wearing tomorrow at the wedding?"

"You might say that." Delphi was going to mention that she was going to drive over to the old farm the women had purchased for the Peace Encampment, but just then Paul clattered down the stairs.

"Dad, is that a speedboat out there? For pulling skiers?" He was goggle-eyed as he jumped down the last step and skidded to a stop in front of his father.

"It is and it will." Micah laughed, feeling an excitement himself at the thought of taking his son out in the boat. "Would you like to try it?" he asked, knowing he should be phoning New York to discuss the Wiedmer contract. He saw Delphi put her hand over her mouth. He leaned around Paul to take hold of her arm and pulled her forward. "And no chortling out of you, lady mine."

Paul raced back upstairs yelling to Dory to get her suit on, that Dad was going to take them out in the boat.

Delphi looked up the stairs from the haven of Micah's arms. "It sounds like they're taking the walls down."

"And the doors and the windows too." He put his hand under her chin and tilted her face so he could look into her eyes. "Are you sure it isn't going to be too much trouble having them in the house for the summer?"

"Not for the summer. Always. I intend to let them choose where they would like to go to school and if they wish to live there or at home. Of course Paul will be starting college, but Dory still has another year of high school. . . ."

"You're good, Delphi." Micah could feel a tightness in his throat as he held her close to him. "And you're my darling; I can't wait to marry you and keep you forever."

Delphi took one of the county roads perpendicular to Route 89 to get to Route 96 where Sally had told her the farm was located.

Driving past the Seneca Depot, she looked at the barbed-wire fencing and the towers with new eyes. She felt an anger that something stored there could threaten the safety of her baby. "Not to mention the futures of Paul and Dory," she mumbled, succumbing to the urge to poke out her tongue at the enclosure. Several miles past the "Seneca dump," as some of the county residents referred to the depot, she saw a hand-written sign that said WOMEN'S ENCAMPMENT FOR PEACE.

She turned in the driveway slowly, looking around her.

There were cars and campers parked at the back of the barns. There were women and children playing, working, talking together.

Delphi stayed in the car, even when a smiling woman gestured to her to join the group sitting on the front lawn.

"Del-fee. Del-fee," Helga called from the front porch, quickly coming down the rickety steps of the farmhouse that was gray with age. "Don't go. Wait. I come to you." The tall smiling blond woman with the coronet of braids came over to the car, putting her hand in the open window to shake Delphi's. "It is good you come, Del-fee. We go today to march in front of the gate."

Delphi's mouth fell open. "You do. Oh, well, you see, I don't think I should—"

Helga's face dropped. "You do believe in what we do, don't you, Delphi?"

Delphi looked at the buxom woman and nodded. "Yes, Helga, I believe in what you're doing . . . and . . . and I'll go with you."

"Good, good. Come, we will tell Sally you're here. Did you see how many people have come this week?" Helga waved her arms at the host of people and vehicles.

"All these people came this week?"

"Most of them." Helga nodded.

Sally walked out onto the porch and waved to Delphi. "Hello and welcome. Mrs. Cramer is coming for the march on Wednesday. It will be larger and we'll have pamphlets to hand out, but today is important too."

"Mrs. Cramer is coming for one of the demonstrations?" Delphi was aghast. "Will she be all right?"

"This is a peaceful demonstration, Delphi. We have no intention that it should be otherwise."

"But it could get out of hand. These things often do." Delphi bit her lip, thinking of the frail old lady with the twinkling gray eyes.

"We won't allow her to get involved if it looks unsafe," Sally assured her. "Why are you here today? We didn't expect you to come." Sally smiled at her.

Impulsively, Delphi said, "I came to ask you and Helga if you would join my family and me at the Gould Hotel for dinner tomorrow evening." Her face reddened. "I'm getting married tomorrow."

Before she could say more, Sally hugged her, then beckoned to Helga. "Married! That's wonderful." She turned to the Dutchwoman who bustled up to them. "Delphi is getting married tomorrow and she asked us to join her for dinner tomorrow at the Gould Hotel in Seneca Falls."

"That's good. We go, huh, Sally?"

"We certainly do go."

"Thank you. Micah will be pleased to meet you and I would like you to meet my uncle. Of course Mrs. Cramer will be coming and my two step-children, Paul and Dory. . . ." Delphi chatted to the women and answered their questions until a woman they called Lois said it was time to leave.

Helga and Sally clambered into the Mercedes as Delphi backed out of the drive and waited to take her place in line.

The cavalcade didn't take long since they were only situated a few miles from the depot.

Delphi parked her car and took the placard that Sally handed her and marched with the women up and down in front of the main gate.

It was peaceful and uneventful and to Delphi's

relief it didn't take long since she knew that Micah and the children would be wondering where she was.

She didn't dawdle after dropping the women back at the encampment and getting their promise that they would be at the hotel in Seneca Falls at seven forty-five the next evening.

She drove back across the county road to Route 89 and down to the beach road, stopping at a road-side stand to buy vegetables and fruit.

When she drove down the lane on the property, she saw Micah. He walked over to the Mercedes and opened the door on her side. "Here you are at last, darling. I was worried. Did you go to get fruit?" He glanced in the back seat and saw the baskets and bags there. He lifted her out into his arms and held her, then he kissed her upturned face, cheeks, lips, and chin. "I hate it when I can't find you."

Delphi stared into the onyx eyes even with her own, since Micah suspended her in his arms. "You were coming to look for me?"

"Uh-huh," Micah admitted, blood creeping up his face. "I find that I'm nervous when I can't find you. I'm afraid you'll run out on me again." The words were low and enunciated as though he brought them up from the depths of his being.

"I will never run from you again. It would be like putting a lance into my jugular vein to leave you," she murmured, liking the warmth of him seeping into her spirit. "I feel one with you now. . . ." She decided to confess to him, knowing the grit it had taken on his part to say what he had. "Sometimes it seems as if we've been married for years. . . ." A new shyness surfaced from within her.

"Now, you're blushing, my darling," Micah said huskily, not releasing her. "I can't believe how we've hidden away from each other all these months." There was a surprised note in his voice. "If anyone had asked me, I would have said that you and I have had a very open relationship."

Delphi nodded, her hands dancing over his hair and neck. "I agree. We had that contract and talked about everything—"

"Most everything." He lowered her to the ground but kept his one arm around her. "Have I ever told you that I hated that damned contract . . . that I've wanted to marry you almost from the moment we began living together?"

Delphi stopped walking, feeling her mouth drop open. "But . . . but you didn't want marriage. We agreed we didn't want commitments."

Micah shrugged. "That changed the moment we began living together. I used to spend hours trying to figure a way to break the contract and get you to marry me. I used to daydream about celebrating our fiftieth wedding anniversary." He grinned at her. "I guess I sound pretty stupid. Oh, baby, don't cry." Micah started to laugh when the big tears rolled from her eyes. He swept her up close to him and hugged her again. "Angel, mine, don't cry." He chuckled.

"I can't help it. It's so beautiful." She dug her fingers into his neck. "Oh, Micah, I used to have nightmares about having to leave you when you grew tired of me and found someone else."

"I hated men who came near you or wanted to dance with you." He set her on her feet again, his eyes a black velvet furnace as they roved over her. "Do you know your lovely round bottom shows so nicely in those cut-offs?" He inhaled deeply. "But I don't like you going out without a bra. Your breasts are too lovely . . ." He scowled when she laughed. "It's not funny, Delph. I can't stand other men looking at you."

"Micah!" She was torn between laughter and horror at his extreme possessiveness.

"You don't know what it's been like loving you." He exhaled a long, harsh breath. "Anyone who doesn't think love is torture has never been in love." He looked down at her, a glint in his eyes. "Casual affairs are easier on the system." He laughed when she punched his arm.

Paul was waiting on the far side of the barn, arms akimbo, watching them. "Do I have to watch you kids all the time? Naughty, naughty . . ." He gave them a cheeky grin. "Parents are not supposed to sneak off into the barn."

"Ahhhh," Delphi said, grabbing him around the waist and tickling him. "Spoilsport."

"Moms . . ." Paul gasped, "stop it."

Even when Delphi ceased her teasing, he didn't step away from her. Instead he leaned down and kissed her cheek.

"What is that for?" Delphi felt a rush of love for Micah's son.

"Because you're a super mom. Didn't you know that?" Paul said, a little embarrassed.

"Me, super mom." Delphi thumped her chest.

"Don't do that . . . even in fun. . . ." Micah took her fist to his mouth. "You might hurt yourself."

"Micah . . ." Delphi half laughed. "That's ridiculous."

"Forget it, Moms." Paul looked at her solemnly. "He thinks you're made of glass."

"More fragile than that," his father informed him.

Paul laughed. "Dad, you look as though you're going to take on the world." He jogged away, still chuckling. "Hurry up, you guys, I'm starting the fire."

"I *would* take on the world for you," Micah said.

Delphi gulped, feeling a tear roll out of her eye.

"Not again!" Micah hugged her to him. "We'll all be swimming up to her necks in tears by the time this child is born."

"Isn't it awful?" Delphi sniffed and accepted the handkerchief he offered her.

Dinner was fun but Delphi was aware that through all the joking and laughter, Micah's eyes didn't stray from her very often, nor did the furnace heat in them abate.

They sat and played five hundred rummy in front of the fireplace after dinner.

When Dory went out to the kitchen to make popcorn, Micah called to her. "Remember! No butter on Delphi's. Hers should be plain."

Delphi rolled her eyes at Paul. "Now he's a nutritionist." To her surprise, her stepson didn't laugh.

"Dad's right, Moms. You should watch the amount of cholesterol in your diet."

Micah shot the stunned Delphi a triumphant look. "See?"

Dory came back in the room to see the two smiling males and grimacing Delphi. "Are they picking on you, Moms?"

"They are planning my diet." She shrugged at the girl who paused a moment, holding two bowls of popcorn.

"That's a good idea. I read an article once that said a woman who encases her baby in fat does it a disservice and that eating properly takes care of that." She pursed her lips and looked at her father. "Of course, Moms doesn't like junk food and she doesn't drink soda."

"She doesn't drink alcohol, either. That's good," Paul inserted.

"I have white wine once in a while and I have been known to drink a Bloody Mary." Delphi spoke up.

"Not often," Micah barked back.

"Good," Dory and Paul said together.

"May I have my unsalted, unbuttered popcorn while the three of you thrash out my life for the next few months?" Delphi fumed.

Dory handed her the smaller bowl, without breaking her part of the discussion on good nutrition and exercise to give elasticity to the uterus and aid in quick and safe deliveries.

"I never heard of that," Delphi said around a mouthful of popcorn, unbuttered and unsalted.

Three heads swiveled her way. Three faces looked at her blankly as though they wondered why she had spoken at all.

"Well, I haven't," she mumbled as her hand clawed into the creamy puffs of corn and lifted more into her mouth. She rose to her feet.

"Where are you going?" Micah barked.

"To get a drink. I'm thirsty."

"I'll get you some ice cold skim milk, Moms. Sit down. Dor, are you sure there was no salt in her popcorn?"

"That's insulting," Dory bristled. "I was very careful to keep hers separate."

Delphi opened her mouth to tell them all to back off, but when she saw the melting looks they cast her way, she gave them a weak smile instead. It was going to be a long pregnancy.

When they said good night to Dory and Paul and watched them go upstairs to their rooms, Micah kept his arm around her waist, his mouth pressed into her hair. His heart seemed to be pumping thick and fast. The mere thought of sleeping with her in the new wing on the new king-sized bed was getting him aroused. When he felt Delphi's hand on his lower body caressing that arousal, he was sure he was going to jump through his skin.

"Is a prospective daddy supposed to be this way?" Delphi crooned to him, snuggling closer as they walked through the door leading into the private hallway to their suite.

"This daddy thinks it's a preferred state," Micah said.

"Good. This mommy feels the same."

They stood in the doorway leading to their bedroom for a few moments looking at the billowing sheers in palest apricot that were tied back from the sliding door window. The quilt on the bed was in circle patterns of turquoise blue, peach, and cream, the same colors repeated in the hooked rug on the random-width pegged floor.

Micah began to undress her, his face flushed, his eyes fixed on her. "Your tummy is so sexy." He swallowed as his hands made slow whorls on her middle. Then he leaned down to kiss her there, his tongue darting at her navel, then lower, his hands grasping her hips.

He lifted his head to look at her, thinking that there never was a more beautiful woman than his Delphi. He tasted the slight salty taste of the skin on her abdomen, his eyes still on her red-gold hair. "Your eyes are a silvery jade, my darling," he muttered, his own excitement deepening as he saw her eyes change color again. How could this woman do such powerful things to his emotions? His chest felt as though it might burst from the pressure of so many feelings. He loved Delphi. Treasured her. Desired her. . .

Eight

The four of them drove to the church the next day.

"I can't believe how relaxed I am." Delphi sighed, smoothing the skirt of the creamy silk dress she was wearing, her fingers then going to the single cream rose she wore pinned at the back of her head where her hair was in a soft twist. She turned around to look at a grinning Dory and Paul. "It must be because you two are here." Then she looked at Micah. "Don't you think so, darling?" There was a silence. "Micah, don't you think so?"

Micah threw her a quick glance, his mouth tight, his eyes narrowed. "What? Yes, of course, whatever you say is fine with me."

Muffled laughter from the back seat turned Delphi's attention away from her puzzled scrutiny of her husband-to-be. "What are you two laughing at?"

"Dad's the one who's nervous, Delphi," Dory said.

"Don't be silly," Delphi murmured, then stared at her love. His hands gripped the wheel at eleven and one o'clock positions. He chewed on his lower lip. His jawbone moved as though it were rock scraping on rock. "Darling," she whispered, sliding across the seat of the car. "You aren't nervous, are you?"

"Dammit, yes, I am, Del. I've never felt like this in my life." He swallowed hard. "And tell those kids to stop smirking. I can hear them."

"Sweetheart." Delphi pressed his arm as he turned off Route 89 to the road that would take them into Seneca Falls. "You've been married three times . . ."

"There is no need to remind me of that. This is different." He paused. "I have never wanted to be married so much. . . ." He shook his head. "I can't explain."

Delphi laid her head on his arm. "I do understand. This day means so much to both of us . . . to all of us."

Father Conroy met them in the church. "Before we begin the ceremony, I wanted to speak with you both . . . no, with all of you, since you will be a family." He smiled at them but there was a grave look to his eyes. "Marriage is a very sacred and beautiful state of man, and in today's society, it is also one of the most disposable items there is . . ." He talked for several minutes about commitment, about caring, about seeing the future as it involved all members of the family, not just one.

Delphi looked sideways at Micah, aware that he took little dictation from anyone. He was too used to being the boss, the declarer of how things would proceed. It stunned her to see him nodding his head, smiling.

At seven in the evening precisely, Father Conroy brought them up to the altar and began the ceremony. Delphi was delighted that the priest did not hurry, but rather took the time to include Dory and Paul as much as possible, even asking them to say a few words as part of the ritual of vows.

Dory was shy and said only a few things. "I hope my father and Moms . . . I mean Delphi, live happily forever. . . ." She blushed when the priest told her that her sincere feelings blessed the marriage more than holy water could.

Paul, on the other hand, cleared his throat and said that he was delighted to have a mother like Delphi and that he had never known his father to be so happy.

Delphi felt she would burst when they repeated their vows to one another. It surprised her when the priest nodded to Micah after the vows and her husband turned to her, taking hold of her hands. "My darling . . ." And then Micah recited the Yevtushenko poem "Colors," pausing only to wipe the tears that wet her cheeks. Then he finished and drew her into his arms for a tender kiss.

They shook hands with the priest, then kissed Dory and Paul.

Delphi stood with her hands clasped, looking around her at the Gothic beauty of the church. "I want to remember everything . . ." she murmured. Then she felt herself caught around the waist by Paul.

"Congratulations, Moms. Whoops, Dory said I was to say best wishes to you and congratulations to Dad . . ." He grinned at her and kissed her cheek. "Either way, I'm glad you're ours, and we're yours now."

"Oh, darling . . ." Delphi sobbed, "so am I." She hugged him to her.

"You mustn't mind Moms, Father Conroy. She's been teary lately ever since . . . owww, Dory, what did you do that for? Don't you know you're in church?"

"Then hush your mouth . . ." Dory hissed at her brother before smiling at the puzzled-looking priest.

"Father, I hope you will join us for dinner at the Gould Hotel shortly." Micah inclined his head.

"Perhaps I will come in time for dessert and coffee, but don't hold a place for me. This is a busy evening for me." The priest smiled at them, gave them his blessing, and the four of them turned to retrace their steps down the center aisle of the church.

"Now, you are mine forever, Mrs. Steele," Micah whispered as he held the oaken doors for her.

"And you're mine." Delphi shivered at the coolness of the late spring breeze.

"Darling, you're cold. . . ." Micah looked grim. "I should have bought you a fur anyway."

Delphi laughed as he wrapped his suit jacket around her. "I have an angora stole in the car, silly."

"You should have furs . . ." he grumbled, helping her into the car.

"You mean you don't have any furs at all, Moms?" Dory quizzed her.

"None."

"She refused to keep any I bought her . . ." Micah barked, making his son give an amused hoot.

"Wow, Moms. You must be the only person in the world who has told Dad that they didn't want his gifts."

"It isn't funny, Paul." Micah shot a black look in the rear-view mirror.

"Yes, it is, Dad," Dory giggled. "Moms, you are wonderful."

Micah was silent as they crossed the river to the other side of town, Delphi pointing out to Paul and

Dory the wide water area known as Van Cleef Lake. "See, that's the Episcopalian Church that sits so close to the water. When I was a little girl I used to pretend that it was a castle, because of all that gray stone."

"It does look like a castle," Paul observed, craning his neck until the edifice was out of sight and they were driving down Fall Street toward State Street and the Gould Hotel.

"If we have time, I'd like to show you the marker on the next corner where Susan B. Anthony made her speech for Woman's Suffrage." Delphi sucked in a breath, recalling that she had intended to tell Micah that she had been to the Women's Peace Encampment and had met the two women who would be joining them for dinner. She stole a glance at her rock-jawed husband who was still irritated about not being able to get her to accept a fur coat. "Ah, darling, wasn't it sweet that Nora and Sam called to say they wished they could be with us? Wouldn't Billy have been cute at the wedding?"

"Cute?" Micah murmured. "He probably would have screamed 'Duhwy, Duhwy' during the whole ceremony."

"What did you say about Susan B. Anthony, Moms?" Dory interjected.

"Ah . . . just that she made her speech here," Delphi muttered, feeling the smile slip off her face as Micah pulled into the parking lot.

Dory nodded, wrinkling her forehead for a moment.

As they were walking toward the hotel, Delphi cast around in her mind for some way to separate Micah and herself from Paul and Dory. She was about to suggest that the youngsters go around the corner and see the landmark sign themselves when Micah intervened.

"We have a few minutes. If you like we can walk around the corner and see the marker."

"Great," Delphi concurred, her brain turning to soggy oatmeal as she struggled to think of another ploy to get him alone to explain her recent activities.

Now it was her turn to be silent as the other three read the historical marker about Susan B. Anthony and her cohorts who began the movement that ended in the law allowing women to vote.

As Delphi searched her mind for a way to talk to Micah for a few minutes, Mrs. Cramer came up State Street, waving to them, and her hopes sank into her sandals.

"Congratulations to both of you!" The elderly lady was effusive as she pushed a package, wrapped in silver and white, into Delphi's hand. "I wanted to give you something meaningful, dear. This silver dish belonged to my grandmother . . . and the family rumor is that she went against her husband's wishes and invited Susan B. Anthony and her friends to tea, serving bonbons in that dish."

Micah kissed the old woman and smiled, his face turned away from Delphi. "Thank you. We'll treasure it. Won't we, darling?"

Delphi swallowed and dredged up a smile. "Oh, indeed we will." She then turned and put her arm around Dory. "This is our daughter, Dory, and our son, Paul."

In the ensuing introductions, she managed to move closer to Micah. "Darling, you think I might speak to you for a moment?"

"That must be Uncle Wilmore and Aunt Jane . . ." Dory grimaced but at a look from her father she was quiet, her face expressionless.

Now they were all clustered in front of the three

steps leading up into the hotel and Delphi had no chance to speak to Micah.

"Hello," Sally called as she and Helga came through the gloom of early darkness from the parking lot.

"Who are they?" Aunt Jane demanded tartly.

"They are friends of mine."

"Oh?" Micah said. "Did you know them when you were a child, darling?"

"Oh, dear . . ." Mrs. Cramer said faintly. Then she hurried forward to speak to the approaching women in low tones.

Somehow the introductions were made, and they all filed up the steps into the dignified building.

Mr. Flynn had their table waiting for them.

Micah stepped back to take Delphi's arm, but when she turned to say something to him, she found that the maître d' was waiting to seat her.

While they had appetizers and drinks and many toasts, Delphi felt reasonably safe. In fact the only thorn seemed to be Aunt Jane.

"Tell me where you're from, Helga. I can't quite place your accent," Micah said conversationally.

"I am from the Netherlands. Rotterdam is my home, but I have been doing much traveling this last year . . . for the cause." She smiled a healthy toothy smile.

Aunt Jane sniffed. "A foreigner."

Delphi groaned.

Mrs. Cramer put one hand up to her mouth and muttered "Oh, dear."

Micah looked around the table then back to Helga. "What cause?"

Sally coughed and touched Helga on the arm. The other woman was too fired up to notice the agitation on the three faces.

"Why, the Women's Coalition for Peace. That is why we are here in Seneca County—"

"Mrs. Cramer entertained us at lunch one day while your wife was there," Sally stated, interrupting her friend, who looked at her with a puzzled frown.

"Wow . . ." Dory breathed. "How many women are here?"

"Hundreds, and many have brought their children."

"And doesn't that upset some of the residents in this area?" Micah asked in a velvet voice.

Delphi knew that voice. He was suspicious, irritated. "Ah . . . there has been no trouble so far. . . ." She coughed and slanted her eyes away from her husband when his head whipped her way.

"No?" he coughed.

"There's been some," Helga pointed out, her lips pursed, shaking off the plucking fingers of her friend Sally. "But we have come to expect some resistance in our work. It is not popular to buck the system, as you Americans say, to swim upstream like the salmon, but we would not be women with a conscience if we did not step forward and speak out against nuclear proliferation."

"I thought the government didn't admit to storing nuclear weapons here." Micah spoke low.

"That's why we're sure they do," Mrs. Cramer pounced, then bit her bottom lip when Micah's gaze slewed her way.

"I see." He looked down at the tablecloth, making whorls on it with his knife. His head snapped up and he fixed his eyes on Delphi. "I won't have you putting yourself in any sort of danger." His voice fired round the table, low, but each syllable was like a missile that made everyone straighten in his seat as though he were the headmaster and the rest of them his students.

"No, darling, I wouldn't do that." It was a relief to Delphi that he knew everything, and she was positive that he did. None of the rest of them could guess at the quickness of his mind, Delphi mused, her eyes loving him, so very proud to be his wife.

Mr. Flynn came by just then to ask how everything was and Micah nodded, then spoke to him. "This hotel has quite a history."

"It does indeed, sir. The first structure on this site was built one hundred and fifty-six years ago. It served the stagecoach trade, the railroad, and the water travelers." Mr. Flynn expounded. "We're very proud of the Gould."

After the man left, Mrs. Cramer gave Micah an impatient look. "I could have told you all you want to know about this hotel. One of my ancestors was Thomas Carr, one of the early owners. He was from England."

"I didn't know that." Sally leaned forward to look at the older woman.

Delphi breathed a sigh of relief that the talk had veered away from the Women's Peace Encampment.

Despite Jane's sour expression, the rest of the evening was an enjoyable one for all.

They drove home that night in the mellow darkness of almost summer in the Northeast, the air like casked wine, full of character and depth, the mild crispness speaking of early summer.

"Do you think we could swim tomorrow, Dad?" Paul yawned.

Micah shrugged, his hand going over to cover Delphi's knee. "Maybe. It wasn't that cold this morning."

"It would have frozen an Eskimo's knees," Delphi interjected.

"Ah, Moms, it isn't that bad. The three of us can swim, then go for a sail. Right, Dory?"

"Not me. The girl I met, Beth Dickers, who lives down the beach road, invited me to go into Rochester with her and her mother tomorrow to shop. I think I'll do that, unless you want me for something, Moms?"

"Would you like to go sailing with us, Moms?" Paul invited.

"No," Micah responded. "She will do her sailing after the baby is born, not before."

Dory giggled. "Dad, you are so funny. Nothing will happen to Moms. Being pregnant is no big deal today."

"That's what I try to tell him," Delphi sighed, turning to smile at the girl.

"Dad's right." Paul stunned his stepmother. "You can't take chances."

"Right." Micah nodded.

"Forget it, Moms. They're ganging up on you. You don't have a chance. You'd better take up knitting." Dory laughed again.

"Needlepoint is nice too," Micah said thoughtfully, making Delphi stare at him, mouth agape.

"Yeah," Paul agreed. "I remember reading where Rosey Grier, the great football player, used to do needlepoint as a tension relaxer. Be good for you, Moms."

"Moms should do needlepoint because the N.F.L. does!" Dory's voice was scathing.

"Lord, I am in trouble," Delphi breathed to Micah as he helped her from the car, the two teenagers walking ahead arguing the merits of needlepointing—in the N.F.L. "Paul will probably have me working out with the Buffalo Bills."

"I can't wait to see you running over the tires, love," Micah whispered, as he hooked his arm around her waist. "How does it feel to be Mrs. Micah Aristotle Steele, my darling?"

"Lovely," Delphi gulped.

"God. Crying again?" Micah chortled.

Delphi smiled at him. "This is my wedding day to the man I love and will love all my days. There is no more important thing in the world than that."

Micah swallowed hard, his throat working up and down. "You say the most wonderful things, Delphi Steele, but I wish you would save them until I have you naked on our bed."

"Ummm, sounds delightful." She closed her eyes for a moment, kissing his chin. Then her eyes snapped open and she laughed.

"What are you laughing at?" Micah bent over her, his voice thick.

"How many parents spend their wedding night with their children?"

"Dammit. That's not funny, woman," Micah growled, stooping to lift her into his arms.

"What are you doing, Micah? I can walk." She looked around her when he passed the back door leading into the old summer kitchen and followed the path around to the front porch, overlooking the lake. "Where are we going?"

"To the front door of our house. I intend to carry my bride over the threshold." He winced for a moment as he heard rock music coming from the second floor. "Even if there are a few changes in the candlelight, champagne, and soft music scenario."

"I love them," Delphi said into his neck. "Sometimes I feel as though I had given birth to them."

"I'll tell you something funnier. I feel that way myself at times." He looked down at her. "You have made Dory blossom as a young woman and both she and Paul love you as though you were their mother."

"I know." Delphi kissed his chin, then called up the stairs to to say good night to her "children." "I never understood what maternal ego was before I had Dory and Paul. Now I do."

"Silly lady." Micah carried her through the door leading to their own apartment, closing the door with his foot. "Do you know, Mama-to-be, you are getting heavier."

"Beast," Delphi cooed, biting his neck.

"Ouch. That makes me sexy."

"Everything makes you sexy," Delphi said as he lowered her to her feet, then began undressing her.

"Correction. Everything about *you* makes me sexy."

"Nice."

"Isn't it?" Micah's voice had a heavy, sensual quality that seemed to press on, then penetrate her skin. "You are silk . . . and velvet. . . ." He kissed her shoulders, then her arms as he undressed her.

"And so are you—a hairy velvet, a rough silk that I love," Delphi babbled as Micah sat her down on the bed and began to roll her stockings down her legs. "I like it when you kiss me behind the knees like that."

"I like it, too, my angel."

"The married couple that plays together—or something like that." She cast around in her mind for the finish of the paraphrase, but her mind went blank as Micah continued his aggressive gentleness. "I like doing this. . . ." Her words were slurred.

Micah's husky chuckle had a tremor to it as he clasped her even closer. "Darling, I hope so. We'll be doing a great deal of it over the next seventy or eighty years. . . ." The thought of his future with her, the long, warm years of having her love surround him, coat him, protect him from the elements that had frosted his life, made him tremble even more.

"We have so much," Delphi sighed as she lay there naked, his gaze fastened to her rounding body. "And you don't even dislike my basketball shape."

"Do you know how sexy you are, lady? Your skin is like satin, and being pregnant has made you more voluptuous than you were when I first met you. You are so sensual that you scare me." Micah caressed her thighs with his lips. "My life would be a desert without you." He lifted his head to stare up at her, his midnight-hued hair mussed where her hands had riffled through it. "It would be the barest survival without you. I wonder if I would have the strength to work, or eat, or even sleep without you."

"My darling Micah," she blubbered.

"Sweetheart, you can't cry when I'm making love to you." Micah looked at her with amused horror.

"I know." She gulped back a sob.

He leaned over her and took her mouth, his tongue entering and teasing hers, loving, demanding, giving.

Delphi felt her pulse beat out of control, the tears in her eyes dry in the hot passion of Micah's love.

Words disappeared as delight with one another built to an intolerable level. Mushrooming passion billowed them out of themselves, lifting them away from the earth and all others.

Micah's tongue and hands slid over her in gentle possession, taking her, but giving more, cherishing her in a ritual that was as strong as their vows.

Delphi felt the power enter her and charge her so that her body became vulnerable yet potent, enervated yet invincible as she took him to her in the clasp of life.

It was several seconds before they could breathe evenly again.

"I . . . I do so very much enjoy that." Delphi could feel a giddy smile stretching her mouth.

Micah shook his head. "You say the damnedest things . . . but I love to hear you say them."

"Good." Delphi yawned.

"Time for all Mamas-to-be to go to sleep."

"Uh-huh," Delphi muttered, her eyes already closed. "I loved my wedding night, Micah. Thank you. 'Night."

"Good night, my darling wife." Micah's chuckle was breathed into her hair. "Thank you."

Delphi woke to sun streaming in the wall windows that had been slid back to allow the balmy lake breeze to enter the room. "It's beautiful." She slithered up on her pillows, a lazy feeling of well-being pervading her as she stared out at the crystal blue water of the lake.

"Yes. It is." Micah stood in the doorway, holding a tray in his hands, his gaze fixed on her, not the beauty of the day.

Delphi could feel the blood running up her neck into her face. "You are not supposed to make a new bride blush," she told him in her primmest voice.

"Can I help it if she makes me feel sexy sitting there with just a corner of sheet covering the lower . . . so interesting part of her anatomy, while the top is so invitingly bare? God, I sound like a poet." He closed his eyes for a minute when she laughed, then opened them, coming closer with the tray. "And you make no attempt to cover yourself, lovely one." He shook his head, inhaling her fragrance as he sat the footed tray across her knees. "Even first thing in the morning, you smell so fresh."

She stretched her bare arms up around his

neck, aware that he was looking at her body again. "Why should I cover up? You would be disappointed if I did that."

"True." He groaned into her skin. Then he lifted his head. "Stop, woman, right this minute. I'm trying to feed you your vitamins and minerals." He lifted the metal covers from the dishes. "I'm certainly glad whoever lived here before believed in stocking hot plates and dishes. They come in very handy when you want to feed a pregnant lady in bed." Micah sounded complacent.

Delphi hardly heard him. She was too busy staring at the laden tray. "Oatmeal with peaches on top." She looked up at him, trying to smile. "I'm not sure whether I can eat it—all." She corrected herself by adding the "all" to her statement when she saw the crestfallen look to him. "But . . . but you could help me . . . with the eggs . . . and ham . . . and bagels and jam. . . ."

"The jam is homemade. Your uncle brought it from his house. He says they never eat all the things his wife puts up. Dory made the coffee cake yesterday and I brought rye toast so that you could have a change of pace from the bagels."

"Are we having guests to breakfast?" Delphi stared at the array of foods as Micah carefully re-covered each dish, then poured her orange juice from a pitcher, arranging her vitamin pills in neat order next to the glass.

He frowned at her. "Don't be silly, darling. Why would we have guests on our very first morning as man and wife? We want to be alone."

"Right, but unless you climb into bed this instant and start having some food, you'll be carrying quite a load back to the kitchen."

Micah needed no second invitation. He lifted the sheet, then paused as he gazed at her body. "You are so beautiful. Your tummy turns me on." He grinned at her when she chuckled.

"Come into bed at once, husband."

At first Micah only fed her, then as her appetite flagged, he began devouring the eggs, ham, bagels, jam, toast, coffee cake, and coffee. "Umm, it's good." Micah looked at her sideways as she sat close to him, their thighs touching.

"Did you ever hear about a woman who became sexy just watching her husband eat?" Delphi whispered.

"No. I don't think I have." Micah wiped his mouth with his napkin and lifted the tray onto the table next to the bed. When he turned back to her, he was already pulling the terry-cloth shirt over his head.

Delphi reached out a hand to pat his hair that had become mussed, her pulse rate doubling as she watched him pull his jeans down his legs. "I want you, husband mine. I want you very much. I think even more than I wanted you yesterday—or the day before that," she mused.

"Good, because I have wanted you so much, I hurt with it." As naked as she now, Micah leaned his head on his hand, his body sprawled close to hers. "All my life I have controlled money, companies, people. I'm used to it. I'm good at it . . . but when you left me, my woman, life went sour. I couldn't make a decision and I didn't want to, I felt hemmed in by my employees. Their faces became grotesque masks." He shook his head, his one hand coming out to rest in the curve of her waist as she lay facing him. "I want you, Delphinium Reed Steele. I want you and need you."

Delphi let her hand feather over the crisp curling hair of his chest, then she bent to kiss the nipples on his breast, smiling to herself when he sucked in a quivering breath. She slid over on top of him, pressing him flat to the mattress. "Soon I won't be able to do this, when I look like a bushel basket."

"I like it when you cover me like a blanket." Micah cocooned her with his arms, his body cushioning hers. "Don't ever leave me—please."

"Never—until you tell me to go."

"That will be when our unborn child is on Social Security . . ." he mumbled into her neck.

"Good." She kissed his nose, watching her hair swing around his face.

His hand came up to thread through her tresses. "The color is so beautiful. Red-gold hair and silver-green eyes. Lovely."

"Well, you have to like it. I belong to you," Delphi explained, nibbling on his ear.

"Do you, my angel? I like that."

The words became scrambled, fragmented as they focused on each other, their sense of touch, smell, and taste, taking over and blanking out the others, swelling their flesh, pumping their blood faster, ever faster.

Micah kept her atop him as they began the love seizures that had their bodies straining together. "My darling wife," he groaned as the power generated by their love took them away.

They lay, holding one another, love sweat slicking their bodies, her head resting under his chin.

"We do have something special, don't we, Micah?" Delphi murmured.

"Very special, my love. My brain tells me that a love like ours cannot be sustained, and yet my spirit points to the fact that I have loved you more each day I've had you." His breath ruffled the dampened tendrils of hair at her temples. "You are my unexpected sunrise."

They fell asleep holding each other. When the

house intercom buzzed, they both came foggily awake, looking at each other.

"That will be Paul"—Delphi yawned behind her hand—"wondering where you are. Sailing today."

"Damn, I forgot. When I made Dory's breakfast earlier, she mentioned that she would be having dinner with her new friend, then we talked about Paul and me sailing today, then I came back to bed with you." Micah shrugged, then smiled at her, even as he pressed the button on the console. "I got sidetracked . . ." he mouthed, then listened as Paul spoke. "Yes, yes, I'm coming. No, son, there's no problem, of course I want to go."

"He's such a good boy," his stepmother said proudly.

"Terrific," his father agreed. "But I would still rather spend the day in bed with you."

"I would like that too." Delphi let him help her from the bed and lead her to the shower. "Then we could have wallowed in the hot tub, made love, then had a cool shower and made love."

"Delphi, stop that," her husband grumbled.

"Awwww," she chided, closing her eyes under the spray of water as she felt Micah shampoo her hair and lather her body. "This is wonderful service, darling, but Paul will be chafing at the bit."

"I wanted to shower anyway. This won't take that much time." He palmed baby oil into her wet body, then massaged it in with gentle strokes. "What are you planning to do today?"

"Ah . . . I thought I'd grill veal scallops rolled around carrots and celery and make stuffed tomatoes and roasted onions and spinach salad with mushrooms. . . ."

"You aren't just preparing food all day are you?" Micah scowled. "I don't want you working hard. We can eat out."

"I like to cook for you." She kissed his nose

before she dried herself and dressed in a cotton shift. The bell-like shape of the dress camouflaged her round tummy, the off-shoulder style was cool for the warm day ahead.

"The paper said this would be one of the hottest summers on record in the Northeast, and it looks like today is going to be a dandy," Micah said, pulling on scruffy cut-offs and a sleeveless shirt for sailing. "Are you going out anywhere?" He looked at the crisp cotton shift in sea-green with white ruching on the neckline, a hot grin creasing his face.

Delphi took a deep breath. "I thought I would drive over to the Women's Peace Encampment."

Micah looked up from tying his sneaker, his eyes narrowing on her. "Honey, I'm not sure that's a good idea."

"Are you going to forbid me to go?" Delphi could feel her chin lifting.

"No. I'm not. I admire your principles, though I can't say I agree with you on this."

"I know you have government contracts . . . and . . . and I don't want to interfere with your business. If you feel that I would be a thorn in your side by going, I won't." Delphi looked into his eyes as he rose to his feet.

"It would be easier on my peace of mind if you were not at that encampment, but I feel that you must never compromise your principles for my business or any other business." He walked toward her and took her by her upper arms. "You're my life. Promise me you'll do nothing that could harm you and the baby."

"I promise," Delphi sniffed, the ready tears coming to her eyes.

He leaned down and kissed her makeup-free mouth. "And I must tell you that ladies who answer a cause do not blubber." He chuckled when she pinched his side. "Darling, be careful driving and take the big car. What time will you be home?" He couldn't hide the worry that assailed him. He wanted to tie her up and put her in that bed and never let her out of the house, but he knew that he would never do that to her. The thought of anything stifling her spirit, smothering her fierce independence, brought a sour taste in his mouth, but he couldn't stem the swell of nervousness at her being at the Women's Encampment for Peace.

"Darling," Delphi breathed, reaching up a hand to smooth the hair from his forehead, "I will be fine. Mrs. Cramer will be there and Helga and Sally and they are very sensible people."

"True." He swallowed. God, it was awful to love someone. Delphi owned him and he didn't mind—but dammit, those soldiers better be careful. "I hate it and I'll think of you all day, but I also know that a person has to be answerable to his conscience." He kissed her hard. "Be careful, love."

"I will."

Paul protested when he heard where Delphi was going. "No, Moms, you shouldn't go. What if somebody gets antsy . . ."

Delphi saw Micah grind his teeth and she leaned over and pressed her hand on Paul's mouth. "Don't worry about me. Go sailing and have a good time. I'll be back before you are."

They finally left.

Delphi stood on the beach waving to them as the strong breeze lifted them out on a wave, billowing their sail, making them scull out as the catamaran skated over the rippling lake.

Delphi went out back, past the barn to the Mercedes parked in the drive.

She had called Aurelia Cramer but the woman said that she would be driving the vintage Oldsmobile that had belonged to her husband.

As Delphi drove down the highway to the county road that would take her over to Route 96, she wondered if women all over the world felt that their efforts for peace were worth the hardships they suffered to get their point across to people.

Nine

The milling women stopped Delphi at the entrance to the driveway.

"Hello, I'm Beryl Deans. You're Sally's and Helga's friend who was just married, aren't you?"

"Yes. I'm Delphi Steele. Are Helga and Sally here?"

"They just left in a big old black car with a Mrs. Crandall, I think."

"Her name is Cramer. I'll just follow along. Are they at the main entrance to the depot?"

"Yes, I think so. Say, would you mind taking some of us along with you in your car? We're a little short of transportation. So many people have joined us in the last few days."

"Of course." Delphi nodded. "I can take five—or maybe six in a pinch."

"Great." Beryl grinned, then turned to wave to some women standing on the front porch of the rather run-down farmhouse. "Come along, ladies. I have a ride for us."

The Mercedes accommodated five people and the chattering entourage proceeded down Route 96 to the front entrance of the Seneca Army Depot. It was a short ride and none of the women seemed to notice when Delphi didn't scramble out of the car as fast as the rest of them.

Men with guns! And helmets! And uniforms! Men in jeeps with heavier weapons! What was she doing here? Delphi asked herself as she stepped from the car, not able to take her eyes from the high barbed-wire fence standing between the women and the military.

Delphi saw other cars too. The blue and gold of the State Police vehicles caught her eyes. She saw the Seneca County Sheriff and some of his deputies. She swallowed, tempted to get in the car again and drive away. Micah was right. She didn't belong here.

"Why don't they tell them broads to go home?" yelled a burly man in plaid cotton shirt.

"Yeah." Another man swiped at the sweat on his forehead with the back of his hands. "What the hell do they know about anything anyway? If my old lady came here, I'd take care of her."

Delphi took two steps, then another, then she was walking by the small group of men jeering the women.

"Hey, lady," another of the hecklers called to Delphi.

She whirled to face him, anger filling her, her hands out in front of her. "You shut your cotton-picking mouth, you bonehead."

In the stillness, Delphi's voice turned heads, some of them military ones.

"You damn well remember that this is a free country and the right of free assembly and protest was fought for and won by the men who wrote our Constitution." She was shaking her finger in the faces of the men. "And if you don't agree with the statement the women are making here, then go home. But don't you dare try to intimidate free citizens of this country. I am a freeborn American." She spun on her heel and walked with her chin high and her knees shaking to the nearest group of women, whose mouths were hanging as far open as the men's.

"Hey, you," the plaid-shirted man began.

"Shut your mouth, Stan. The lady's right," one of the other men said.

There were a few more rumbles but slowly the shouted remarks and angry epithets died away.

When Delphi walked over to the women who had ridden in her car, some of them took hold of her hand and shook it.

"It was nothing. Ah . . . Beryl, did you say this was where Sally and Helga were going to be?"

The other woman craned her neck, swiveling her head this way and that, trying to see over the crowd. "Yesss, I'm sure they're around here somewhere." Beryl shrugged. "I didn't expect this many to show up today."

Delphi put her hand on the other woman's arm. "Don't bother yourself. I'll just wander around and look for them."

"All right." Beryl looked relieved. "Thanks for the ride—and for having the guts to speak up to that guy. There aren't too many like that, but then again, it only takes a few to start a full-scale melee." Beryl squeezed her arm and faded into a milling group of women.

Delphi moved slowly along the fence, worming her way through the throng, smiling at some who spoke to her and nodding at others. She took note of the many placards stating the women's aversion to proliferation of nuclear arms.

She wandered quite a ways, then saw some women down a small gully near a culvert. She stared at them and thought that one of the gray-haired women looked like Mrs. Cramer. She ambled down the shallow gully and approached the group. When she was almost there she saw that what she had thought was gray hair was in fact a platinum blonde who turned and looked at her, putting her index finger to her mouth, then waving Delphi closer.

"Come closer. We'll give you a leg up." The blonde nudged another woman who turned, listened to the blonde and nodded.

Delphi looked at their expectant faces, their hands clasped to make a cradle for her foot, then up at the barbed-wire fence. She could make that, she thought, patting her tummy. One of her specialties when she was a child was the ability to scale any fence with ease without touching the wire or the wood. "All right, but take it easy when you heave me up there. I have to take care of myself."

"We're the best heave-hoers in the encampment. Right, Berta?"

"Right." As the woman bent forward, Delphi saw the cross hanging from her neck.

"You're a nun?" Delphi quizzed, putting her left foot on their crossed hands.

"No, but I'm married to a minister. There are quite a few nuns here, though."

"Hurry, we have to get her up and over and move on to the next bunch," the blond woman urged.

Almost without thinking, Delphi took hold of the wire mesh as she felt herself hoisted. She grasped the pole with the gloves the women had given her to wear and swung her leg over the top. For a moment she was poised there and to her horror she saw a jeep with two soldiers coming down the road that bordered the fence.

"Hurry . . . hurry. Get down before they see you. The women along the way are distracting them but they can only do that so long," the blond woman urged.

Delphi climbed down the other side, feeling exhilarated by the experience. She looked around her, then back to the other side of the fence. "What am I doing here? What should I do?"

The blonde laughed. "Just walk around. Being inside like that, you are making a statement that you don't approve of the storing of nuclear weapons."

"I don't." Delphi smiled weakly when the others waved good-bye and went down along the fence. She turned, then saw the jeep coming her way. Instinctively, she hid behind some bushes, running across the road and toward another side road leading through the compound.

To her surprise the men in the jeep went on by.

Delphi wandered along one of the roads, looking around at the rather uninteresting topography. It was flat and not appealing.

She had been walking for about a half-hour when she saw the two-story buildings that she recognized as the homes for the enlisted personnel.

She stood there wondering if she should approach them and ask directions to the front gate, when she heard the screech of brakes and the rattle of gravel behind her.

"Ma'am, I would be obliged if you would come with us, please." The helmeted soldier with an M.P. banner crisscrossing his chest stepped out of the jeep and approached her.

Delphi swallowed, lifting both hands into the air.

"If you would just get in the jeep." The man helped her into the back seat and then sat next to her. "You are being held by order of the United States Army, ma'am."

"I see." Delphi wished all at once that she had stayed home. She had never even had a parking ticket. Now the United States Army wanted her.

She was taken to the main gate where trucks were parked and being loaded with other women. She was about to walk toward a truck when she saw Mrs. Cramer on the other side of the front gate waving to her.

"Sally and Helga are in that truck you're in, dear. I tried to climb the fence but I couldn't . . ." Aurelia Cramer gave her a rueful smile.

Delphi heard her name again and blinked into the sudden darkness of the truck. "Sally," she breathed, relieved, feeling teary when Helga rose to her feet and hugged her. "I hope we can get out of here before Micah finds out where I am." She huddled between the two women, listening abstractedly to the scattered conversations of the other occupants of the vehicle.

When it rumbled out the gate, Delphi felt herself thrust against Helga. "Where are we going, do you know?" she whispered to Sally.

"I heard someone say that they were taking us to a school. South Seneca was the name, I think." Sally put her arm around Delphi. "Don't worry, we'll probably be released right away."

Delphi nodded. "Sure we will." Oh no, we won't, she moaned inside. God, Micah will have a fit.

The ride wasn't too long, but far enough and bumpy enough so that when they arrived, climbing down from the vehicle was rough.

"God, I'm stiff." Helga groaned, taking Delphi's arm. "Are you sure you are feeling all right? I should have told you not to come. Being pregnant can be very delicate."

"I wanted to come and I am healthy as a horse," Delphi assured her, looking askance at the brick school building, then following behind the other women who were being shepherded through a door.

The echo chamber sound in the corridors of the school rang through Delphi's mind as she nodded her head and went into one of the schoolrooms.

They were there about forty-five minutes when a captain came into the classroom. "Ladies, you will be detained overnight."

The rest of what he said faded from Delphi's mind. Overnight? Here? Dear heaven!

"Don't look like that, Delphi. It will be all right, you'll see." Sally patted her back.

"Sure." Delphi smiled weakly. *Micah will shred me into bite-sized pieces and I don't blame him.*

Helga leaned over. "Listen to me. Diane Metters just told me that the bathrooms are not guarded. . . ." When the others would have spoken, Helga shook her head and frowned at them. "Say nothing." She turned around and watched several women go out of the room, saying they were going to the restrooms, then they would return.

Almost all of the women had gone out and returned, when Helga looked at them, nodded, then stood walking slowly to the front of the class. "Going to the bathroom."

The soldier nodded.

Another soldier watched the three of them go down the hall as four others were returning to the room.

"We do not go in there, until we see three of them come out, then we go in," Helga hissed, slowing her walk.

One woman came out. The three of them walked closer to the few women queuing up for the bathrooms. When three women walked out, Helga pushed ahead of the others. "Excuse us," she muttered. "She's sick to her stomach. Just follow us in after a few minutes." She stared at the women, until one of them nodded.

Helga jerked her head at Sally and Delphi, pushed open the door, then followed them in. "Do either of you have to use the facilities?"

"I do," Delphi said, then studied the other woman's tight face. "I can wait."

"Good." Helga walked over to the window, tried pushing it up. The heavy window stuck.

Both Sally and Delphi pushed, to no avail, then Sally took the old wooden window pull and propped it under the wood. The other two women pushed. With a sudden *whush* the window was up.

Sally rushed to flush one of the toilets, then Helga climbed on the sill, looked around her, then dropped to the ground.

Delphi went and flushed another toilet, then Sally climbed on the window and dropped out of sight.

Delphi was about to flush the toilet again when the door opened. The woman stood there, motioned to someone behind her, put her hand over her mouth and went to the booth and flushed the toilet. "Get moving," she said to Delphi.

"Thanks." Delphi climbed on the sill, but didn't jump. Instead, she turned and lowered herself down the brick face of the building. She felt one of her friends grasp her legs. "We have you, Delphi," Sally whispered.

Delphi let go and fell into her friend's arms. "Sorry," she gulped, out of breath, but feeling very good.

"Do not dawdle." Helga lifted Delphi to her feet with one strong pull. "We will walk away as though we are some of the spectators."

"I'm ready." Delphi giggled, then covered her mouth. "I haven't had a day like this in years, but I feel good. I feel we have done something. The best part is, that Micah won't know how I was detained," she babbled.

Sally squeezed her arm. "I'm just glad we did get you out of there. From now on, you just support us in principle."

"Ja, that's true." Helga grinned. "I was so scared when I saw you get in the truck. I am afraid to ask how you got over that fence."

"I'll tell you . . . someday . . ." Delphi stopped speaking as they approached the corner of the building, taking a shaky breath as she looked over Helga's shoulder at the noisy crowd in front of the school, a line of soldiers across the sidewalk.

Helga looked back at them. "I will go first. Then you will come, Delphi. We must be . . . be . . . how you say it . . . easy."

"Casual is a better word." Sally grinned, giving the thumbs up sign to her friend.

The two of them watched Helga stroll up to the crowd of people, then stand with them and look toward the school just as though she were an onlooker.

"Now, Delphi . . . go . . ." Sally pushed at her back.

Then Delphi was walking forward, trying to keep her face blank, her eyes on the school building.

She thought she had made it. In fact, she was about to turn around to see if Sally was behind her when she felt a hand on her arm. When she looked down and saw olive drab, she gulped and turned.

"Weren't you one of the women we took inside just a while ago?"

"I b-beg your pardon." Delphi tried to inject hauteur into her voice but there was a reedy sound to it anyway.

Others in the crowd looked their way. Delphi saw a grimacing Helga stalking toward her.

"Now look here, lady, I don't want to get tough, but . . ."

"You damn well won't get tough with her," Micah roared, flattening the grass with the power of his anger, trees bending before his thunder. "Take your bloody hands off her, or I'll take that billy club and bend it round your jaw," Micah vowed in clear, well enunciated syllables.

People backed away until there was a cleared space with Delphi, Micah, and the unarmed soldier in the center. To Delphi's foggy mind, it was as though time had stopped.

An officer came forward, a placatory smile on his face as he viewed the scene. He opened his mouth to speak and Micah whirled on him.

"Tell your soldier boy to take his hands off my wife, or I will dislocate his hip from the ear down." The hissed words sailed around the grounds like missiles, making the circle bigger as more people retreated from the wrathful black-eyed bear. "He's got two seconds. . . ."

"Micah . . . darling . . ."

"Now see here, mister."

"One . . ." Micah crooned.

"Release his wife," the lieutenant barked.

Delphi found herself scooped forward into Micah's arms, her face pressed into his shoulder. "I'm fine, darling, really I am."

Micah didn't stop his scrutiny of the soldiers, but his hands clenched on her as her breath teased his neck. "These women have a right to protest and assemble to do so," he instructed.

"Your wife climbed the fence into the depot," the officer explained.

Years of boardroom infighting stood Micah in good stead as his face froze over, masking the deep shock he was feeling at the thought of Delphi climbing a fence. "Must I remind you lieutenant, that she is a citizen of this country, a taxpayer, and as such she has every right to protest. I'm taking her home, and you damn well better release the others." Sweeping her up into his arms, he strode through the milling people like Moses through the Red Sea.

Delphi's head bumped against his shoulder as his long strides carried him past Mrs. Cramer. "Good-bye," she called to the elderly woman.

"Good-bye, dear. It was nice, wasn't it?"

"Yes," Delphi answered. "Ouch," she whispered to her husband whose hands were digging into her.

"I should spank your bottom," he grated as he set her on the front seat of the car and closed her door, then came round the front of the car, his scowl scattering the many interested onlookers that had clustered nearby.

"Micah? Darling?" Delphi tested the waters.

"How dare you climb a fence?" The car shot out of the parking spot and down the street, flinging Delphi against her seat belt. Micah saw her body move out of the corner of his eye and slowed, his right hand going out to her abdomen and resting there. "You could have injured yourself . . . the baby . . ." Micah's voice was hoarse.

"Darling. I was perfectly safe."

"No! You were not safe! My God, when that lieutenant said that you had climbed the fence . . ." He swallowed.

"Not all by myself. Some women boosted me up to the top and I swung my leg . . ."

"God," Micah groaned, one hand punching the steering wheel.

Delphi saw it through his eyes for a moment. "Darling. It was stupid. I'm sorry. I'll never do anything like that again."

"You're damn right you won't." Micah ground his teeth together. "We are leaving here today. Your Uncle Wilmore is staying with Paul and Dory at the cottage until they return to our home in New York. They tell me that you have already told them that you want them to come and live with us and that they would like to do that."

"Yes, but where are we going?"

"On our honeymoon. I have a great deal of talking to do with my wife."

"You do?"

"I do."

"Micah, are you terribly angry?"

"I'm angry with myself for allowing you to get in that sort of fix."

Delphi took hold of his arm, sliding herself close to him. "Micah, you couldn't have stopped me. I believe in what the women are trying to do—but I don't want you to have adverse publicity because of it."

"Damn the publicity—and my businesses." He swiveled his head her way for an instant. "I would not have stopped you from making any statement you wanted to . . . any written statement, but I would have stopped you from climbing that fence."

"Darling, that was the loudest statement I could have made in protest against nuclear arms."

"Not true. I own a magazine, a chain of newspapers, and an advertising firm. You could have used any and all of them to make your statement. YOU still can. I will buy you billboards in every major city in this country with your words on them."

"Yet you believe in nuclear arms, don't you?" Delphi whispered.

"I have, yes." He smiled at her, then looked back at the road. "I have interests in some companies that use nuclear power. Amtron Electronics, one of my subsidiaries, has a government contract for switches used in nuclear submarines." Micah shrugged. "It seemed to me it was just a wave of the future, part of marching forward. But . . ." He held up his hand when Delphi would have spoken. "I also feel that my wife has every right to speak out against any and every cause she chooses and I will support her every way that I can."

"Even letting me broadcast my views that do not coincide with yours?"

"Yes, my sweet, even that—and there will be no time limit or limit on the amount of money you can spend ever." He swung down Oak Beach Road, the car purring over the few ruts in the pavement.

"Micah . . ." Delphi choked, shaking her head. "I don't understand you sometimes."

"I know that now. That's why I'm taking you away. Tomorrow, my darling, we will sleep in the apartment in New York. Then we fly to Greece to my home on Delos, where we will be alone, to talk, to love, to think." He parked the car behind the barn and came around to open her door and help her out. "You do not know how much I love you yet, but you will."

"Micah . . ."

"Moms!" Paul shouted, galloping across the grass between the house and the barn. "We were worried." He skidded to a stop in front of Delphi, then put his arms around her, hugging her. "Don't scare us like that."

Delphi felt a honey sweetness at the concern she heard in Paul's voice. She hugged him back, then leaned back to look at him, feeling the tears on her cheeks. "My baby."

"Aw, Moms, you're not going to cry again, are you?" Paul grimaced as his father laughed. "Boy, Dad, when you take her to Greece, you'd better make sure that none of the staff see her crying." Paul drew the back of his hand across his throat.

"True. Archimedes and his wife will no doubt adopt her at once." Micah looked at his wife, the heat in his eyes coating her skin.

Dory and Paul were going to stay at the lake with Wilmore, who brought Jane to dinner that night. The evening went well and—like a miracle—Jane even laughed once at something Micah said.

After they left and the children went to their rooms, Micah put his arm around Delphi. He led her out onto the silver-dappled beach, the stars and the moon glittering over the water.

"Tonight is the last night that you will not understand what you mean to me, my wife. Tomorrow when we fly to New York, then on to Greece, you will begin to know what you truly mean to me."

Ten

The flight to New York from Syracuse Airport didn't take as long as the cab ride into Manhattan.

By the time they reached the apartment, Delphi felt a relaxed sleepiness.

"I told the housekeeper to put a casserole in the oven. We'll have wine and rolls, then it's discussion time, my one and only wife."

"Micah, darling, you have had three other . . ."

Micah turned her in his arms when they walked into the kitchen, after dropping their luggage in the front hall. "My darling Delphi, you are the only woman who has ever captured me, opened up my veins, climbed into my body and taken it for your own. Never forget that."

"I won't."

Micah kissed the tip of her nose, grinning at her bemused face. "You don't understand me yet, but you will, my love."

Delphi watched him check the oven, then the refrigerator.

"All set. Let's go up and shower and get into those Oriental pajamas."

"Ohh, I love you in that kimono," Delphi growled at him, then laughed.

"You look pretty good yourself in that black-and-turquoise silk. God, let's hurry, I'm getting aroused just thinking about you dressed that way."

Delphi chuckled, sighing as she leaned against him as they went upstairs to their own suite of rooms. "I can't believe I'm a married lady, expecting a child."

"Are you happy?" Micah asked her as he stripped the clothes from her.

"Uh-huh. You've given me two beautiful children already and I will have another one . . ."

"Five months and a few days," Micah growled into her thigh as he rolled the stockings from her legs.

"That computer brain of yours. . . ." Delphi ran a hand through his hair.

"Darling." Micah chuckled. "You think anyone who can balance a checkbook is a master mathematician."

"And so they are." Delphi glared at her husband. "Why do you think they have banks if it isn't to balance checkbooks? It's silly for a person to try to do the job of a bank."

"God, your analytical reasoning astounds me," he teased her.

Delphi surged to her feet, aware that his eyes were on her naked body. "So what do you want? A calculator or a voluptuary?"

Micah rose to his feet, his nostrils flaring as he stared at her. "You are what I want . . . you in any guise you choose, but always you."

"Micah . . ." Delphi held out her arms to him.

"Yes, my darling, I'm here." Micah lifted her up the front of him.

"There is something I would rather do than shower at the moment." Delphi plucked at the hair on his chest.

"Oh? And what might that be?" The onyx sheen of his eyes made the gold and brown flecks glisten like jewels.

"I have a hankering to wrestle with my new husband," Delphi drawled, the upstate Yankee twang in her tones.

"I will resist all advances." Micah lowered her to the bed, kissing her throat, his mouth sliding downward to the swell of her breasts.

"This is resistance?" Delphi squeaked.

"Yes, a very subtle variety, guaranteed to keep you on your toes." He nibbled at the soft underside of her breasts.

"My toes are curling," Delphi gasped. "Does that mean I'm on my toes?"

"Smart lady, aren't you?"

Repartee disappeared as electricity jarred them loose from their ties to earth and they began that zooming climb toward the sensual plane where they were one.

Micah entered her with a gentle fierceness, his heart pounding out of control as he felt her body surround him and take him deeper into her. There was no one in the world like Delphi! And now she was his wife!

Long moments they lay on the bed in each other's arms, wanting the closeness to go on, neither one willing to break the velvet fetters that bound them to each other.

Micah felt her wriggle on his chest and looked down at her upturned face, marveling at the luminescence of her skin, the childlike, fragile bone structure of this woman who looked at him with such love. I can't ever lose her, he thought. If I do, it's over, the sunshine, the whole "colored" world.

"What are you thinking, Micah?" She yawned behind her hand, then smiled at him.

He eased her off his chest and sat straight up, stretching. "That it's time to remove the casserole from the oven and set the table." He stood, turning to face her, loving it when she looked at him. "Stop that, wife. You're doing it again." He turned and left her when she laughed, awed at the way she could arouse him, even after the rousing, satisfying love they had just shared.

He was shampooing his head, his eyes closed against the run of soap down his face, when he felt the draft of the shower stall door opening. "Come in, darling." With eyes still closed he opened his arms to her, his heart thumping when she pressed her satin skin along his form. "Shall I wash you?"

"Yes, please. Since I have known you, Micah, my showers and baths have doubled."

"Mine too," he said huskily, his hands busy in her hair, loving the thick red-gold glory of it, as the wet darkness of it slid through his fingers. He felt his hands tremble when he washed down her body with the loofah sponge she preferred to the facecloth.

He dried her with the same concentration, trying to still his pulse when he patted her derriere dry. He couldn't resist bending forward and nipping the luscious curves with his teeth.

"Micah!" Delphi giggled. "Stop that."

"I've never heard you giggle." He led her to the huge wall closets that housed their things, a warm terry towel wrapped around her.

"I don't think I've ever felt so carefree." Her head dropped to his shoulder as she watched him reach for the silk pajamas that she would wear while they dined.

"That is what we are going to talk about, my sweet one. All about your freedom, your life, your happiness . . ."

"Oh? That must mean that you're going to talk about you, then, because that's what you are, my freedom, my life, my happiness." She made the declaration in a serene, relaxed way.

Micah felt poleaxed. His insides exploded. Words formed, then melted in his brain. Thought splintered and faded. "No one has ever made such a commitment to me, Del."

"My life is yours, Micah." She shrugged a shoulder as she preceded him from the room. "I didn't want it like that. The contract we signed said that we would always be free agents whenever we chose, that we only had to inform the other when we wished to terminate the arrangement . . ." she recited as they crossed the hall with the balcony overlooking the foyer and began to descend the stairs. "We wouldn't have children, nor would we in any way encumber the other, our lives would be free, so that each of us could carry on with our own lives and careers as well as be with each other."

Micah took her hand when they followed the long hall back to the kitchen. "Now that agreement is null and void. We broke it when we married and made our new contract with each other."

Both set the table and while Micah removed the casserole from the oven, Delphi made the salad.

"I think still wines agree with you more than champagne," Micah observed, pouring a crisp Chablis into the tulip glasses.

"Unfortunately, my insides are plebeian." Delphi pressed her hand on middle. "My baby wants beer, not bubbly."

Micah frowned at her as he pushed her chair forward, then took the one at right angles to her. "I'm glad you don't like alcohol too much. All the articles and books I've read on childbearing consider booze a risk in large amounts."

Delphi choked on her wine, staring at him as he put a large portion of shrimp and rice on her plate. "You've been reading books on childbearing?"

"Yes. I bought some at the little bookstore in Seneca Falls."

"But, darling, you've had two children. It's no mystery to you."

"It was not frightening to me when Dory and Paul were born. This pregnancy scares me. I don't mean to take any chances with you."

"I'm fine. I couldn't be better." Delphi watched him openmouthed.

"Close your mouth, eat your food, and drink your milk." Micah was testy with her. "Stop looking so surprised that I would want to take care of you."

"Darling . . ." Delphi began, her words soft, "I'm not surprised that you would want to take care of me. I just don't think you need to get that involved. . . ."

"Involved? What the hell does that mean?" Micah thrust his jaw out, his voice rising. "I am the father. I'm damn well involved with this baby and I damn well am going to stay involved."

"Yes, but . . ."

"No buts, Del." Micah bellowed the ultimatum.

"You never used to yell like this," she observed, her chin on her hand as she watched her husband clear the plates, march to the kitchen like a drill sergeant, then return with the deep-dish raspberry pie the housekeeper had provided.

"I do not yell," Micah stated, his voice a muted roar. "But I will not have you trying to minimize my role in the life of our child."

"Is that what I'm doing?" She looked at him as he leaned down and lifted her from the chair and carried her through to the living room.

"Yes—and that is why we are going to have our talk, and then tomorrow we are going to Delos and we will talk to each other and make love and plan our life which will last at least sixty more years. After that if you feel you want to be free of me, we'll negotiate, but not until then."

"Oh." Delphi looked at him as he sat down beside her on the huge U-shaped couch in front of the fireplace. "It looks like my liberated days are over," Delphi observed with a mixture of amusement and horror.

Micah turned to face her. He cleared his throat, his arm along the back of the couch, close to her but not touching. "Wrong, my darling. You are in full charge of our lives from now on. The only thing you cannot orchestrate is our separation at any time." He stood up and went out of the room for a moment.

Delphi heard his study door open, then in a few minutes close again. She watched him, feeling a serene joy that she was in the same room with the man who made the earth spin on its axis for her, who brought soft summer rain and glistening sunshine into her life, who made her grow, weep, laugh, and savor all of life.

Micah came back in the room, his broad-shouldered strength having a litheness that many smaller men could not match—his ebony eyes and hair a glistening complement to his lightly swarthy skin that had a tan year-round, which never needed a sunscreen.

Delphi sighed, leaning back on the couch. "You are one beautiful man, Steele."

He paused before sitting down beside her. "I love it when you talk to me that way. You are the only person in the world who could ever dent my ego, darling, but I think you know that." He tossed a legal-looking sheet of paper on her lap.

"No. I never knew that." Delphi was honest with him. "I thought I was the vulnerable one in our association."

"Did you, angel?" Micah stretched himself out on the couch, his head on her lap. "Read our new agreement."

Delphi glanced at the paper, then put it down on the couch, her other hand sweeping his crisp, slightly curling hair back from his forehead. "Why don't you tell me what it says, instead of my reading it." Her voice was low as she bent over him and rubbed her lips over his cheek, an almost invisible bristle appearing even though he had shaved a little over an hour before they ate.

"All right." He lifted a lazy hand to put a strand of her red gold hair into his mouth, sucking on it gently. "It says in essence that there will be no divorce between us—ever, no separation, not even for a night."

"Even under emergency situations? What if you are stranded somewhere when you are on a business trip?"

He removed the strand of hair from his mouth, his eyes fixing on her as she bent over him. "There will be no more business trips, or any other traveling if you are not with me. That is another part of the agreement. I will have my office wherever you choose to live—even in summer when you wish to be at the lake, Steele Associates will be operating out of Oak Beach Road."

"They will?" Delphi asked, awestruck.

Micah nodded. "They will. Our children have decided they will live with us and go to school nearby. They're happy that, at last, they have a real family life to enjoy. And they want to enjoy the baby."

"Oh, Micah." Delphi trembled.

"No crying, my love, you might drown me," he teased when she leaned over him and hugged him.

"You will dictate where we go, whom we see . . ." Micah recited.

"Micah . . ." Delphi gasped. "I can't do that. That's a decision for both of us."

"You will decide where our homes should be, if you want us to belong to clubs or do not." He covered her outraged cry with a gentle palm. "In other words, that legal document tells you, my darling, what I have been trying to tell you since the day I met you, but because of my bad track record, you would not have trusted my words."

"I have always trusted you, Micah," Delphi gulped.

"I know, in most things you have, but you have always thought that what we have between us was a nebulous thing, with no future, no ties, no long-lasting, deep, deep love on my part. All these long months I have been trying to tell you that I have no freedom, no business power, no smarts of any kind, no wealth, no health, no strength, no love of living if you are gone, my darling. I am repeating myself when I say that you are the unexpected sunrise of my life. I didn't know that life could be so full, so sweet, so awesome. I don't care where we live, what we do, as long as we are together, as long as you allow me to take care of you, you can become president of Steele, or do any other job you prefer."

"Micah!" Delphi was stunned. "I want no part of running your companies or . . ."

"You should, darling. After all, according to the new agreement you have forty-nine percent of all I possess, free and clear."

"Aaagh." Delphi gagged. "No. I don't want it. You

can't give it to me." Her hand flexed in nervous fashion on his chest. "I don't want to be rich," she whispered to him. "It makes me uncomfortable. Put the money in Paul's name—or Dory's. I would prefer that."

"Darling. They have their trust funds, as does our unborn child, but I am not giving our children money, out of hand. They will work their way to money just as I had to do, and you, their mother, had to do. Don't you think that's healthier for them?"

"Yes, but . . ." Delphi was agitated.

"Not to worry, sweetheart, you'll do very well at the board meetings. I'll be there to support you," Micah soothed.

"Micah . . ." Delphi wailed. "This isn't intelligent."

"It's the most intelligent thing I've ever done. You are my darling, my love. We will be together in all we do. What is mine is yours, just as my body and soul are. It is the best move I have ever made. Is there anything you would like to add to our contract?"

"Huh? Me? I . . . I think you must have covered it all," Delphi said faintly.

"Good. Let's go to bed. I want to make love to you and the plane takes off at eleven tomorrow. I don't want you tired for the trip."

"God forbid I should be tired." Delphi followed behind him, dazed. "Micah, why don't you give me just a small portion . . ."

"Hush, my sweet. I have love on my mind and don't want to discuss mundane things."

"Gotcha," Delphi muttered as her husband swept her swelling body up into his arms and carried her up the stairs to their suite of rooms.

Lovemaking reached a new dimension with

them as each strove to give more to the other than ever.

"How can it be better each time?" Micah's guttural murmur went unanswered as his mouth coursed down her body in slow searching wonder, his tongue touching and finding every nerve end in her body.

When they said "I love you" in unison, it was brand new, an untarnished vow never spoken by anyone else.

"I give you my life, Delphinium Steele, all that I am or that I can ever be, to hold in your hands forever." Micah watched her with glassy-eyed fixity as he entered her body with loving hesitancy.

"You need never fear again that 'the unexpected sunrise' will finish, my darling man. I am yours for infinity," Delphi pledged as her body embraced her man. The rhythms of love caused them to soar beyond reach of the world.

Four months and two weeks later, Delphi went into labor when Dory and Paul were home from school.

"You had better let us call Dad, Moms," Paul told her, his brow creased in worry. "He'll have a fit if we don't."

"Paul's right," Dory gulped.

"Don't be silly. I am not due for another two weeks—and first babies can be late, you know, so this is probably false labor. He hasn't been down to the office in over a week and there are many things he has to do. If I'm still this way at dinner time then I'll talk to him about it."

Her children nodded but neither of them left her.

When her back pains became excruciating, she began the breathing regimen that she had rehearsed in the classes she and Micah had taken together. "Perhaps you should call him, Paul."

After Paul left the room on the run, the pains seem to increase.

"Moms . . ." Dory rose to her feet in alarm when Delphi groaned.

"Call a taxi, dear, and call the number that Micah has jotted next to each of the phones. Don't be worried, Dory," she called to the girl as she ran from the room.

Paul came back, out of breath. "Moms, he went out to the plant on the island. They're calling him now."

By the time the taxi came, Micah hadn't been contacted.

For some reason, Delphi felt calm and all during the ride she comforted Dory and Paul. At the hospital she was taken so quickly through the swinging doors that she hardly had the opportunity to say good-bye to them.

"Most impatient to give birth, aren't you, Mrs. Steele?" the masked and gowned doctor asked her. "Or perhaps it's the babies who are impatient. I don't think they want to wait for your own doctor."

"Babies? Aaaah . . ." Delphi groaned, thinking she might not have heard correctly. "Did you say babies?"

"That's right, pant, pant, pant," the doctor instructed.

Micah arrived as the second child, a girl, was being born. He was capped and gowned. "Darling, you did it alone. You didn't wait for me." He tried to joke with her, but fear swamped him as he looked at her pale face, the lines of tiredness etched around her mouth and nose.

"We . . . have . . . another . . . boy . . . and girl

. . . Micah," Delphi told him, reaching up a limp hand to touch him.

"Yes, dearest, I know. God, I love you," Micah's voice broke as he bent over her and pressed his face to hers.

Ten weeks later Delphi and Micah went back to Delos for a vacation, the twins in the doting care of four nurses—two for day, two for night—a sister and a brother, Uncle Wilmore and Aunt Jane, and Mrs. Cramer, who had vowed to stay for three weeks to make sure that Jane was up to par, and not a nag to Paul, Dory, or the nurses.

They slept in the bedroom that overlooked the wine-dark sea, the myriad Greek smells of oregano and basil wafting on the night breeze.

Arms around each other they watched the moon dapple the glittering water. They had made love once, now they stood and watched the magic of the night at the open French door leading to the terrace.

"I will never fear the night again, because you, the unexpected sunrise, will be there for me," Micah murmured into her hair.

"And you will be there for me, my darling, to color my life and give it substance. I'm content."

THE EDITOR'S CORNER

There is a very special treat in store for you next month from Bantam Books. Although not a LOVESWEPT, I simply must tell you about Celeste DeBlasis's magnificent hardcover novel **WILD SWAN**. Celeste has demonstrated to us all what a superb storyteller and gifted writer she is in such works as **THE PROUD BREED** and **THE TIGER'S WOMAN**. So, you can imagine with what relish I approached the reading of the galleys of her latest novel one weekend not too long ago. I couldn't put **WILD SWAN** down. I wrapped myself in this touching, exciting, involving story and was darned sorry when I'd finished that last paragraph. I'll bet you, too, will find this epic tale riveting. Spanning decades and sweeping from England's West Country during the years of the Napoleonic Wars to the beautiful but trouble-shadowed countryside of Maryland, **WILD SWAN** is a fascinating story centered around an unforgettable heroine, Alexandria Thiane. And the very heart of the work is an exploration of love in its many facets—passionate, enduring, transcendent. **WILD SWAN** is a grand story, by a grand writer. Do remember to ask your bookseller for this novel; I really don't think you'll want to wait until it comes out in paperback!

And now to the LOVESWEPTS you can look forward to reading next month.

In **TOUCH THE HORIZON** (LOVESWEPT #59) Iris Johansen gives us the tender story of Billie Callahan, the touching young madcap introduced last month in **CAPTURE THE RAINBOW**. On her own at last in the mysterious desert land of Sedikhan, Billie is driving her jeep toward a walled city when she is rescued from a terrifying sandstorm by a dashing figure on a black stallion. He sweeps her into his arms and steals

(continued)

her heart. Shades of the Arabian Nights! Those of you who've read many of Iris's books in the past will recognize some old friends and thrill to the golden-haired, blue-eyed hero whose kisses send Billie spinning off the edge of the world. This lively adventure tale may be Iris's most wonderful love story to date! Don't be too frustrated now that I haven't given you the hero's name. It's a surprise from Iris. And do let me tantalize you with just a few words: he's a poignant character introduced in an early work and through letters I know many of you have complimented Iris on his creation, rooted for him, taken him into your hearts. At the end of Chapter One, you'll know his name and, I suspect, you'll be cheering!

One of the pleasures of publishing LOVESWEPT romances is discovering talented new writers, wonderful storytellers who bring us their unique insights into the special relationships between men and women. This month we're introducing two of our most exciting new discoveries: first, BJ James, whose novel **WHEN YOU SPEAK LOVE** (LOVESWEPT #60) offers an intense, dramatic and touching romance with a truly endearing cast of characters. While it was heartbreaking tragedy that brought Jake Caldwell and Kelly O'Brian together, what followed was the nurturing of a special kind of love between two people who've longed for closeness but have never known its intimate joy. We think you'll agree that BJ's first novel for LOVESWEPT is beautifully and sensitively written, a truly memorable debut.

Our second "debutante" brings a delicious sense of humor to her first LOVESWEPT romance. Joan Elliott Pickart may be **BREAKING ALL THE RULES** (LOVE-SWEPT #61) in this irresistible confection, but you'll be delighted to join in the fun! Blaze Holland and Taylor Shay both vowed they weren't looking to fall in love that wintry day in New York City, but the stormy weather wasn't the only thing beyond their control. Blaze is one of the most unforgettable heroines we've seen in a long time—and Taylor the perfect foil for her headlong tumble into the arms of love. These two give a new romantic flavor to the notion of popcorn as a potential aphrodisiac! Was falling in love always this much fun?

When you're looking for someone very special, what's the fastest way to find him? If you're Pepper, the resourceful and constantly astonishing heroine of **PEPPER'S WAY** (LOVESWEPT #62), you place an innocently provocative ad in your local newspaper that's sure to compel the perfect candidate to respond! Kay Hooper has done it again with this beguiling and whimsical tale of loving pursuit. Thor Spicer answers the ad and suddenly finds himself the object of Pepper's tireless fascination. He's never met a dynamo like this lady before, and his goose is definitely cooked! **PEPPER'S WAY** is a delightfully romantic story, brimming with the unpredictable twists and turns you've come to relish in each new book by Kay Hooper. Perhaps I shouldn't reveal this, but I've always fantasized about having certain of the unusual talents that Pepper reveals to Thor and his friend Cody in this absolutely wonderful love story!

Whew! September positively sizzles with romance that won't fade at summer's end. It's great to know you'll be there to share it with us as the leaves turn those glorious shades of red and gold!

With warm good wishes,

Sincerely,

Carolyn Nichols

Carolyn Nichols
  Editor
LOVESWEPT
Bantam Books, Inc.
666 Fifth Avenue
New York, NY 10103

WILD SWAN

Celeste De Blasis

Author of THE PROUD BREED

Spanning decades and sweeping from England's West Country in the years of the Napoleonic Wars to the beauty of Maryland's horse country—a golden land shadowed by slavery and soon to be ravaged by war—here is a novel richly spun of authentically detailed history and sumptuous romance, a rewarding woman's story in the grand tradition of A WOMAN OF SUBSTANCE. WILD SWAN is the story of Alexandria Thaine, youngest and unwanted child of a bitter mother and distant father—suddenly summoned home to care for her dead sister's children. Alexandria—for whom the brief joys of childhood are swiftly forgotten . . . and the bright fire of passion nearly extinguished.

Buy WILD SWAN, on sale in hardcover August 15, 1984, wherever Bantam Books are sold, or use the handy coupon below for ordering: